The Lusty Man

The
Lusty
Man

TERRY

GRIGGS

The Porcupine's Quill

CANADIAN CATALOGUING IN PUBLICATION DATA

Griggs, Terry.
The lusty man

ISBN 0-88984-159-4

I. Title

PS8563.R54L8   1995   C813'.54   C95-931563-2
PR9199.3.G75L8   1995

Published by The Porcupine's Quill, Inc., 68 Main Street, Erin, Ontario NOB ITO, with financial assistance from The Canada Council and the Ontario Arts Council. The support of the Government of Ontario through the Ministry of Culture, Tourism and Recreation is also gratefully acknowledged, as is the support of the Department of Canadian Heritage through the Book and Periodical Industry Development programme and the Periodical Distribution Assistance Programme.

Represented in Canada by the Literary Press Group. Trade orders are available from General Distribution Services.

Readied for the press by John Metcalf.
Copy edited by Doris Cowan.

Cover is after a photograph by Howard Schatz/Graphistock.

For my mother, Janet
and my brother, John

And for my pals

The annals say: when the monks of Clonmacnoise
Were all at prayers inside the oratory
A ship appeared above them in the air.

The anchor dragged along behind so deep
It hooked itself into the altar rails
And then, as the big hull rocked to a standstill,

A crewman shinned and grappled down the rope
And struggled to release it. But in vain.
'This man can't bear our life here and will drown,'

The abbot said, 'unless we help him.' So
They did, the freed ship sailed, and the man climbed back
Out of the marvellous as he had known it.

– Seamus Heaney

In the Name of the Mother, and the Daughter, and the Holy Terror

THE BIRTH WAS quick but the christening took forever. Baby Stink was practically walking by the time everybody got their cowlicks battened down and the shit scraped off their heels. *What a family!* was all Ruthie could say. She might have cooked half a Stink in her belly but she sure wasn't one of them. *Never!* She was a Stronghill to the core and slapping on a Stink name, dirty as an old apron, wasn't going to change that. She had Grade A, top-of-the-line Stronghill blood running in her veins, flowing like blue ribbons through her body. Stronghills didn't mess around. You had a baby to baptize, then lickety-split you got him done. Like the way Ruthie made the beds, *snap snap*, with the corners tucked in sharp and tight. Let the Stinks whine all they wanted to about the sheets being like straitjackets, bending their toes at right angles, pointing south. *To hell with them.* What did they know about right angles anyway, they were Stinks. Dead from the neck up. And yeah, what if Baby Stink *died?* The angels would dribble his pudgy little soul, roly as a ball, straight to Limbo, and he'd be lost there forever in a dank and jumbled clutter of nameless things. Those drumbling, mulish Stinks. Just try to coax them into their forty-year-old suits – like coaxing a twisted coil of snakes back into their old moulted skins – and see what happens. What happens? Why naturally Grampa Stink eats all the mothballs he discovers in his pockets and has to be carted off to Emergency. At the hospital they pump his stomach, operate on his cataracts (in case he takes a notion to eat any more of those 'round peppermints'), and since he's in town, might as well remove his troublesome gallbladder, and for good measure top him up with Warfarin because his slinking creeping Stink blood has coagulated into a mess of blobs and clots that moves through his decrepit carcass like mud. 'Can't have a christening without Grampa,' they all say, looking shifty, and scatter in umpteen different directions. *Blah! Stinks!* Slower than plugged bungholes, yet you try to get your hands on one and he'll slip like water through your fingers.

When Grace Stronghill found out her daughter was marrying a Stink, *oh boy*, she ran through the house pulling on her perm and saying *no no no* like she was having a nightmare. 'Fried dog,' she warned, on one of her revolutions through the kitchen. 'Hawkmeat. Boiled mouse.' Off she went again, then reappeared, orbiting through the saloon-style doors faster than an old seventy-eight. 'You name it, dear, and a Stink will eat it. What do you *think* happened to Fluffy Wolinski?' Her hair was curled bright and stiff as chainlink, but was taking a real beating. 'They'll *relieve* themselves anywhere, you know. That bush out front? Rose of Sharon, got the cutting from your grandmother? Lovely, remember? Stinks killed it. Can't seem to pass by here without cocking a leg.' Gone. Back again. 'Oh sweetie, I can't believe you'd *do* this to us.' Ruthie was getting dizzy. 'And something else, they've got this lard bucket right in the middle of their kitchen, and they all gob in it, even the women.'

'Gob, mother? *Gob?* Have you been playing pool at Snappy's again?'

'*Things* happen out there, Ruthie, I'm warning you, everyone knows it. Wife-swapping, incest. And honey, *my God*, they put wallpaper on the ceiling.'

But hey, Ruthie thought, get a load of this: *Mrs Gram Stink.* As she saw it at the time that name lay before her like a soft slithery dress, utterly enticing, and she was dying to try it on. She could almost feel the sheer sensual fabric of the name, how it would splash down her back, how it would cling to her and ride against her. She smiled defiantly, lips pressed smartly together, her one Stronghill dimple engraved in her cheek like an open-ended bracket. The Stronghills were a fine fox-eyed family, long on looks, but genetically tight-fisted when it came to the finishing touches. Missing from Ruthie's features were the charming and unexpected misalignments, the aberrant moles and clefts that were the punctuation of unforgettable beauty. Although between her and her sister Liz, they *did* own a complete set of dimples. If they stood side by side you got the full cutie-pie effect, two smiles contained in a single parenthesis. Gram liked to poke his pinkie into Ruthie's and *ha!* that's not all. But Stink lore? Ruthie had heard those stories since she was a kid, wildly embellished tales of what they ate and drank and did out there in Stinkville, as their sprawling mess of an extended family farm was called locally. It was a proven fact that the Stinks were as thick as bricks and yet the real kicker here, Ruthie knew, was how they once outwitted a Stronghill, way back when they first drifted onto the island like gypsies selling horses they'd dyed with bootblack and henna to cover the grey hairs. Ruthie's great-grandfather, some half-blind horse-mad old stick named Humphrey, bought every last knock-kneed cross-eyed jade, and even threw a rocky chunk of land into the bargain. A year later Humphrey's horses had all toppled over, stiff as planks, while the Stinks sold their land to a mining company and with the proceeds bought a huge tract of farmland in Belchie Township into which they sank a tangled wayward mass of roots. Crooks. Trash. Say what you want about them, was Ruthie's then unsullied and untested opinion, but they sure knew how to make boys. Never mind that the hands they ran up your neck through your hair smelled like dog food, there was just something about those young male Stinks, *Lord*, that made your eyes pop out and your body say *howdy!*

Yeah, well, Ruthie had a Stink boy of her own now, a bawling brawling feisty lad with a flying shock of hair black as smoke. And *eat?* He'd latched onto Ruthie's breast with a low animal growl, slurping and smacking, a true Stink at the trough. Ruthie had to dig out the earplugs she kept on hand for those clamorous Stink suppers – all that chewing and sucking. If only they'd keep their traps shut for once the goddamn half-eaten peas wouldn't keep popping out of their mouths and getting stuck in the butter. Baby Stink had already graduated to solids; he was eating his way straight up the food chain, consuming it as he went. It seemed every time Ruthie turned around, she'd find a chocolate-covered doughnut shoved in his mouth, or him unwinding a great swath of jellyroll, applying himself to its contents with rapt attention as though it were the Book of Revelations. He had burst clean out of his christening gown ages ago. A rag anyway. A baptismal relic that every Stink had worn since they'd crawled out of the swamp, but all it amounted to, as far as Ruthie could see, was a bit of cotton and lace held together with diaper pins and baby puke.

'Fat tub,' pronounced Granny, old LaBelle Stink, who hid behind a blind of senility from which she occasionally shot a verbal dart.

Ruthie leapt to her son's defence, determined to protect him from this kind of lowdown, mean-spirited criticism. The Stinks were always at each other's throats, name-calling and nagging, gouging one another with sharp, hurtful words. How could they stand it? The Stronghill girls were raised on 'Honey' and 'Sweetie' and

'Darling,' a rich confectionery of names doled out generously that laid no rot in the heart. Well, *she* wasn't going to put up with it, she wasn't going to take any lip from that old enema bag. 'It's *boring* being a baby,' Ruthie snapped. '*You* should know. Besides, he has to do something while he's waiting for his family to pull their feeble wits together long enough to get him christened.'

'Lard ass,' shot Granny Stink.

Privately, Ruthie complained to her sister about Baby Stink's alarming growth. 'No really, Liz, I'm getting tennis elbow shovelling food into the kid. What an oinker.'

'Awwww.' Liz tweaked one of his chins. 'C'mon, Ruthie, he's cute. Stick a cigar in his mouth and he'd look like, you know, Churchill.'

'Stick a cigar in his mouth and he'd swallow it.'

'Seriously though, think of it. *Winston*. Winston ... Stink!'

Right, just what Ruthie needed, one more name to deal with when streams of them spilled out of people's mouths daily and flew around her head like ticker tape. And what was the use? Not one of them would stick without holy water, without that good old baptismal glue. Winston, was it? Liz would pick a name like that, a cut above the rest, a name that wouldn't be clipped short or stubbed out like a butt. An old-fashioned name, but unusual enough to give the boy an edge, something to grab onto, an elegant handle to raise himself up with in the world. Funny, nobody was much interested in Ruthie's pregnancy – 'Hey, Nits, how come yer walkin like a duck?' Gram said – but when it came to naming the baby they all wanted to get their two cents' worth in, the Stronghills as pushy as the Stinks. Grace Stronghill was actively lobbying for the name King – her maiden name – as if she needed to see it alive again, inscribed in him and shouted out lustily by him, her forsaken and long-lost name returning to her faithful as an echo. The countless number of times you speak a child's name, Ruthie thought, in rebuke or tenderness, each time a stroke, a loving touch, or a warning shove, a reproving slap. You had to be careful naming a child. Or maybe it didn't matter, maybe they heard the same thing no matter what, the sentiment buried in the name. *Lovie* if they were lucky, or more likely *fool* and *stupid* draining into their innocent ears like sludge down a sinkhole. Personally, Ruthie didn't know if she was ready for *King* Stink, a dubious kind of royalty at best, and anyway King was a dog's name.

Dolly Stink, her mother-in-law, was pressing hard for *Elmer*, which Ruthie considered cruel, it amounted to child abuse. Might as well stamp his face FARMBOY and get it over with, then rush down to Cronk's General Store and buy him a lifetime supply of clod-hoppers and hats with ear flaps. And, of course, Gram favoured a country-and-western bent to a name – a Hoyt, a Conway or Waylon – but Ruthie gave him the evil eyeball whenever those woeful choices came up and he knew he'd better not push it.

So what did Ruthie herself expect in a name, what on earth *did* she want? Obviously, like any mother, something that was a good sensible fit, that would cleave comfortably and adorably to his cuddly bouncy baby fat, and later, when that fat had been redistributed and moulded into a handsomely built hunk of a man, she wanted a name that would adorn and triumphantly celebrate him. *But*, Ruthie realized, if they didn't deck him out in that name soon, the only other name that would ever fit him was Trouble. Already he'd grown rangy and wild, beyond holding in anything too restrictive, and he'd developed a terrible temper. He'd nearly killed Grandpa Stink by bonking him on the head with a rock that he had been sucking furiously on – a dry unyielding breast. (*Ho-hum*, back to Emergency.) Mind you, Baby Stink had reason enough, as Gram was the first male Stink in the annals of that illustrious clan ever to change a diaper, and you've never seen a Stink work so fast in your life, afraid his brothers would catch him at it. Which meant that Baby Stink was constantly being pricked and jabbed, and a few times ended up with the diaper pinned directly onto his leg and screaming bloody murder. Ruthie now absolutely insisted on inspecting Gram's handiwork, which made him peevish. He stuck out his lower lip as he worked, concentrating hard but all thumbs, like somebody trying to dress a beach ball in a three-piece suit. Gram accused her of simply wanting to get an eyeful, peeking in the baby's diaper like that – the boy was clearly destined to please the ladies – but that was Gram for you, jealous even of his own son.

Not that he had to worry. Ruthie wasn't like the other Stink wives, sneaking out of one brother's bed and into another's, carefree and frisky as otters, as though in marrying into the family you got a package deal. That wasn't Ruthie's style, her eyes didn't need to roam. She'd had her sights fixed firmly on Gram since he was a scrawny kid in grade nine tumbling off the school bus with a lunch pail the size of a tool box. She didn't waste *any* time.

'You a Stink?'

'Yeah. What of it?'

'Nothing. Want to go steady?'

'Uhhh, sure. Why not. What do I gotta do? Hold yer hand and stuff?'

'Yeah. Here.' Ruthie held out her hand to him like it was a contract and he squinted at it warily, trying to read the fine print.

After that, Ruthie never wanted to look elsewhere, and for her pleasure – maybe this was part of the bargain – Gram grew these gorgeous shoulders, and the height to support them, and the kind of face that gave you whiplash just snapping your head round to see it, and thick black hair to lose your hands in, and those deep brown, dreamy Stink eyes that, *aaah*, looked right back at her.

You could walk into a room and feel the heat if Gram was in it, as if somebody had left a burner on, or started a fire in the corner. *Crackle, crackle.* That man made Ruthie's nerves dance, her bones hum, her blood bubble and spit, he thrilled her so much. Not that she always showed it. The very first time, years ago, when they really got down to it in his old man's beat-up Dodge, Ruthie nearly laughed her head off. Gram had his underwear on backwards and somehow that struck her as the funniest thing she'd ever seen. 'Honey, your Fruit of the Loom is pointing the wrong way,' she said, and that struck her as being pretty funny, too. Gram got so embarrassed he shoved her out of the car and peeled off down the road, gravel popping and spinning into the air like whole notes, a lively score for the expletives that were streaming out of the car window. Ruthie lay in the ditch along with the empties and rusty tin cans, Queen Anne's lace bobbing above her head, spilling moonlight down into her face, her lips curved like a bowl catching silver. She knew he'd be back. And sure enough, before long a hunched black shape came rattling and clunking down the road, creeping along like a giant slug in reverse, both tail lights smashed out. It occurred to Ruthie even then that the Stinks spend about as much time going backward as they do forward, and that marriage into the Stink clan probably would be – and *was* – like a three-ring circus, complete with the animal acts and the clowns. But Gram, well, *Gram*, he was a promise kept, a promise most gloriously and abundantly fulfilled. When he jumped out of the car that night to gather Ruthie up out of the ditch, his underwear was long gone, nothing left but a spectre of white snagged on a chokecherry branch on the corner of Concession 9, Lot 13 in Belchie Township, and some big crazy bird could make a flag out of it and fly it sky high for all he cared.

But those damn devious Stinks. Wouldn't you know it, the moment Ruthie slithered down, submerging herself in a nice hot tubful of water, settling on the bottom like a rock, something got her, grabbed her by the ear and yanked her up. What *is* that noise, she wondered, some kind of uproar outside, car horns blatting and blaring? A wedding? Had Chet Stink stopped humping his girlfriend long enough to get hitched? Nah. Ruthie jumped up to peek out of the porthole – the Stink bathroom had a nautical decor, including an extended family of fish hooks stapled to the wall to hang their smush-bristled toothbrushes on. 'I can't believe it,' she said, as a lucent stole of water slid down her back. 'I *cannot* believe it.' Below, a procession of vehicles – cars, trucks, a harvester, a tractor, and a motor home – were idling in the driveway, each one crammed to the seams with Stinks. Not just your everyday Stinks either, wearing baggy-assed blue jeans and sweaty faded madras shirts, rolled at the cuff and unbuttoned to the navel. No, these Stinks were dressed to the teeth in new string ties and snappy suit jackets, the women in party dresses and prom gloves, earrings the size of fists, their hair teased high into bales. Baby Stink, who was wearing some gaudy fringed outfit that made him look like a souvenir pillow from Niagara Falls, was nestled in Gram's lap, his chubby cherub hands pounding the steering wheel of the Dodge, *ready to roll*. They were all ready to roll and craning their necks to gawp up at her, that cocky snip of a Stink smile warping their chops.

'Yo Nits,' Gram shouted out of the open car window, 'you comin', er what?'

Ruthie was so mad she punched a hole through the porthole screen. 'For God sakes, Gram, you *could* have let me know. Just *wait* here. DON'T MOVE! I'll be right down.'

Ruthie wasn't a dolt (she wasn't a Stink). She understood how shocked her family must have been, her mother gasping audibly, when she appeared in church with wet tangled hair, oddly paired shoes, her damp dress stuck to her rear end like cellophane, and her underwear sticking out of her purse. '*Nice*,' her sister Liz whispered as she hustled past. Ruthie had planned on sneaking into a confessional to finish dressing, but once the Stinks had gotten this idea of a christening into their heads, like a pack of hounds sinking their teeth into a steak, there was no stopping them. The Stink brothers had already rousted out Father Finn, who still had sleep in his eyes and coffee grounds in his teeth, and who stared with such unfeigned amazement at Ruthie that in response her nipples poked like pinkies through her thin filmy dress and pointed straight at him. He dropped his missal in the baptismal font and splattered her with holy water that tingled on her skin, she thought, like champagne. 'Christ!' he said. And then continuing in a more pastoral tone as he fished out his book and wiped it off on his vestments, 'Yes, Christ is with us today to welcome a new lamb into His flock.' Baby Stink immediately began to screech, as if a zipper of pain had undone him from top to bottom.

If only Ruthie could have gathered up her son right then and whisked him safely out the door. Or if she could have loosened the bonnet strings that were cinched around his neck like a noose, or unhooked a few buttons on that abysmal, bargain-basement, asbestos-lined christening gown that was making him so hot – she could just see the chrism sizzling on his forehead like grease on a griddle – then she might have successfully reined in the skittish sacramental day, saved it from breaking loose and trampling them all under its hard punishing heels. But oh no, she watched helplessly as he was borne away from her on a wave of Stink hands. Stinks considered themselves to be experts in the infant pacification department, Stu Stink had a crenellated head to prove it. Gram told her that whenever he and his brothers got a bit rowdy as boys, Dolly would pop a couple of oranges into her socks, tie the tops together, and go after them like a bolas-wielding cowgirl. 'You know, you can punch a kid through a phone book and it won't leave a mark,' she mentioned to Ruthie in the way of advice when Baby Stink was born. To be fair, they also employed more enlightened and entertaining forms of persuasion, and truly there was nothing quite like being in a room full of Stinks who were all wiggling their ears, crossing their eyes, making fish faces and playing peek-a-boo through stands of yellow nicotine-stained fingers. At least the Stronghills took a more dignified approach, and whenever Baby was even slightly unhappy they would apply a soothing verbal balm, massaging him with soft emollient phrases, a cooing and calming language distilled into a tincture of vowels which they dropped into his ears like a warm healing oil. But try as they might, Stink and Stronghill alike, nothing seemed to work. They passed him back and forth like a hot coal as he continued to scream, wailing in toothless blue-faced fury, arching his back until he was stiff as the statuary that surrounded them. Tennessee Ernie Stink, who fancied himself a magician since he'd picked up his magic kit from the Eaton's order office, somehow managed to pull a boiled egg out of his nose, brandishing it in the air triumphantly to enthusiastic Stink applause, and then he ate it. This enraged Baby Stink *even more*. He seemed to be on the point of consuming himself with fury, when his Aunt Liz Stronghill descended like a fairy godmother, bat-wing sleeves flapping, and divested him of his strangling bonnet and prickly gown. She peeled him quickly like that egg Tennessee Ernie swallowed whole, and set him free. Gurgling happily, Baby Stink crawled away under one of the pews.

'Ah,' said Father Finn. 'We'll catch the little devil in a minute. But tell me, Ruthie and Gram,' he adopted a more solemn tone, 'what *name* do you give your child?'

Rats. This was it. Ruthie realized that the irritating words that had buzzed out of the priest's mouth were inevitable and unavoidable. The subject was bound to come up sooner or later. It was written in the books, as inescapably fated to happen, she supposed, as that incident last summer when a dragonfly darted into Aunt Phyllis's mouth, never to emerge, during an outdoor gleeclub performance of *Oklahoma!* As Ruthie recalled, Phyllis had been giving it her best shot, too, belting it out in the passionate, full-throttle, open-jawed glory of the chorus, when the dragonfly, with a kamikaze purity of intent, plunged into the moist black abyss of her throat and – 'OOOOHHHK-K-K-K' – she choked. No one knew what to make of it. Such a peculiar end. Ruthie could only assume that it was one of those curious inexplicable details in the divine programme, a bit of filigree work on the Creator's part, a deviant riff, a haunting little variation to keep them on their toes, to keep them riveted to that ongoing all-renewing spectacle called life. So of course Father Finn *had* to ask, no matter the consequences. It was, after all, the touchstone of the whole service, the very reason they were gathered together.

Ruthie appealed to Gram for inspiration, hoping that the perfect name would appear sudden as a vision to fill the annoying blank his face was making as he conveyed her own clueless look back to her. Father Finn raised his eyebrows, Gram shifted his feet, and Ruthie shrugged, a series of slight and almost imperceptible movements that nevertheless slashed open the issue from tip to stern, making a deft cut in the tensely held and pregnant silence through which a birth of names tumbled. Everyone began bidding at once, pitching names of every description at the priest, some curt and cornified, blunt as stones, others soft and mushy as decayed fruit. *Willard* came his way, and *Cash* and *Ozzie* and *King*, and *Elmer* for Heaven's sake, and *Porky* and *Beelzebub* (did Grandpa Stink really suggest that?) and '*Hank!*' Burton Stink, Gram's dad, hollered from the back of the church where he'd gone for a smoke, 'The boy's name is Hank.'

'But, Mr Stink,' Father Finn called back, 'Hank isn't a saint's name.'

'The *hell* you say, Father. Then I guess you never bin to Nashville.'

'How about Sebastian?' a Stronghill cousin suggested. 'The child might go in for archery when he's older.'

'Fag's name.' This was Chet Stink. A glum expression had jelled on his face like cold gravy. A brooding dangerous look Ruthie recognized from the time he air-conditioned his trailer with a shotgun.

'There's Denis.'

'Wasn't he the one who carried his head to his grave?'

'*Who* was it, though, that was sawn in half and dismembered?'

'James? Simon? Grumpy? Uhhh, Sneezy? No, wait, that's not right.'

Preserve me, Ruthie moaned, and glanced up at the altar. Christ was clearly suffering. And where had Baby Stink gotten to anyway, the young martyr of the occasion? She strained to look around and over the increasingly restless and agitated bulk of Stink heads and waving arms and angry stolid bodies that blocked her view. She couldn't see him but got an impression of his whereabouts from the way the stiff upper lips of her family would quiver faintly as he groped and pulled himself along a Stronghill row of legs. He had been having a pretty good time worming his pudgy fingers, wiggly and destructive as tent caterpillars, into the women's stockings. He had poked numerous holes, raised several itsy pup tents, and had inched his fingers as far as he could up the sprouting ladders to the waxing and waning cotton-bottomed moons above. He then tried to gnaw the sugary glaze of varnish off a pew, and tore some pages out of one of the delectable books made of rustly golden-edged ciga-rette paper, which proved finally to have so little substance. Leviticus churned in his empty stomach, producing more in the way of gas than satisfaction. He might have packed it in right then, curled up into a ball heavy as a fieldstone doorstop and fallen asleep at the Holy Family's feet, if a tiny hook of light hadn't snagged his eye, a bright tongue licking and licking, lapping up the dark like a cat slurp-ing up a bowl of cream. Baby Stink crawled closer, fascinated with the quick beauty of it, how the baptismal candle flickered and danced, wondering if he might just be able to pull himself up and make a grab for it. He had watched his Stink uncles playing with fire often enough, passing their fingers slowly through a lighter flame, a game to test their mettle, to see who was the bravest (or *stupidest*, his mother said). And only last week Uncle Tennessee Ernie had tried to *swallow* fire, a trick he was working on involving a barbecue fork and a blazing marshmallow, and Uncle had hopped around the room yelping and gagging. So Baby Stink wasn't a complete innocent, he knew this to be a forbidden element, this fiery and seductive tongue that spoke to him, whispering like the Holy Ghost, saying his *true* name, saying *Come to me, come and I will anoint thee.*

But those *hotheads.* Those *goons.* Ruthie didn't know either who had given the first shove, thrown the first punch, or body-checked Saint Anthony so hard that he flew off his pedestal, hands clasped in prayer, and hit the floor like a high-diver, cracking open his head and sending his halo rolling off down the aisle like an escaped training wheel. But *who else?* Who else would start a knockdown brawl in a church? Who else would pop a priest on the nose? Who else would try to drown his own brother in holy water, holding his head face down in the font until that brother repented over some long-forgotten grievance about a runaway bride and a motel in Sudbury? Who else *but a Stink* would usher in dissension so keen that it cut through family lines tough as sinew, that it made even the Stronghills short of temper and snappish with each other? *Who else* would goad her mother, *her own mother*, into calling *her*, Ruthie, a 'slut'? A *Stink slut*, no less. Incredible, but this was the name Grace Stronghill called her daughter, the defiling insult she hurled at her in the heat of the melee like a handful of mud. Grace and Ruthie were both astonished as the unthinkable and unsayable took shape in front of them, divisive as a confessional screen so clotted with sin and filth that no word, no matter how desperately contrite, could penetrate it.

'Look,' someone shouted. And, 'Holeee Christ,' as a wispy unwinding braid of grey smoke rose off the top of Granny Stink's head like an ascending flue of straggly undone hair.

'*Fire!*' someone else yelled.

'Fucker,' said Labelle Stink, giving something at her feet a sharp kick. 'You *little* fucker,' and her old voice crackled dry as kindling and exploded in a red hot shower of sparks high above their heads, before she herself went up in flames.

Strange Gifts

THESE ARE THE things he imagined about himself: that he had a syrinx, the vocal organ of songbirds, lodged in his throat like a hollow bone, like a flute. That he had luciferin in his blood, a light-producing substance found in the bodies of fireflies and certain sea molluscs. That he had elves' eyes, nicked and angled for insight and far sight and mischief. That he had red hair. That his name was Corbin. He did not imagine any of these things about himself to be *true*. Unless he set fire to his hair it would remain an undistinguished mutt brown, dry as sticks. His eyes were unremarkable and conventionally shaped, and his vision merely adequate, although a good pair of glasses might have given objects at twenty feet a more precise and crisp definition. When he sang along with the Top 40 on his car radio, he sounded less like a songbird than a raptor preying upon the squealing fleeing notes in the open field of the melody. His name was Innis. He was driving north in a red Triumph sports car, the thumping body in his trunk actually a body of literature, a corpus of papers and books that slid and crashed from side to side as his toy of a car took the curves at a hundred miles per hour. On his dashboard, where a regular guy might have placed an empty coffee cup or an air freshener, or a grass-skirted pink plastic hula dancer, he had a crudely carved stone penis sitting upright on its balls like a trained seal. Now *this* was strange. But true.

Holmes Stink fished deep in his pants pocket and retrieved a miscellany of objects the lake had given him: a small silver sundial, a rusty skeleton key with a crown-shaped handle, a blue medicine bottle, a brass belt buckle, a shard of porcelain plate, the heel from a child's shoe, the lower left jawbone of a cat. He handled these gifts with the kind of respect one might reserve for relics, those spiritually fecund and proliferating wristbones, canines, and kidney stones of the saints. With careful deliberation he placed them on the metal table before him, and began to observe them with a gradual descent into complete absorption.

First, the cat. *Felis domesticus* stretched from its jawbone to its full skeletal length, rewired itself with nerves, a fresh infusion of blood, grew skin and fur (a familiar, midnight, cross-your-path black) and sweet pointy ears, and weed-green eyes that stared at Holmes with keen suspicion. It leapt high into the air and vanished with a hiss. Holmes stroked the bone lightly, clothing it with his hand and wondering why the crew kept a cat on board, the unluckiest of creatures, next to a woman, to take to sea. They should have eaten the rats themselves and tossed the green-eyed demon into the lake. Not that Holmes would have done this himself, for his heart was a terrain of accommodating soft spots, one of which fit exactly the Esperanto-smooth bit of the skeleton key, the cruel tongue of the belt buckle – the rending stories *it* could tell – another the plate shard with its broken blue garden sown across the lakefloor, and yet another the thorn-sharp heel of the unknown child's shoe.

Imagine a brig schooner one hundred and ten feet long, with a square stern, a double mast, and a hand-carved figurehead with painted wooden eyes watching the wind ruffle the lake, lifting the black waves like the ornate organdy hem of a funeral dress. Imagine the terror on board when the full force of the gale strikes, when the waves rise to twenty, thirty feet, and the ship is locked in a watery prison, unable either to go forward or to retreat into the harbouring safety of a cove. Think of the child ripped by the wind out of his mother's arms, orphaned instantly as a snapped mast crushes her head, the child's name still warm in her mouth, the cradle she made of it praying for him. The ship comes to rest seventy feet under, the tiller and the wheel broken on the stern deck, the side railings cluttered with deadeyes and mounts for the belaying pins, the one mast missing, but beyond that it is in perfect condition. The figurehead still watches as the water undresses the child – utterly – for bed. Leaving only this, this little heel from his shoe.

Holmes has been known to make himself cry, inconsolably, face buried in his big generous hands, just thinking about things that probably never even happened.

One time he found a woman's nightgown delicately draped across a jumbled pile of timbers, ghostly white in the underwater gloom, luminous as snow. It was laid out as though waiting for its owner to swim out of the darkness and put it on. Holmes picked it up and held it billowing open to him. Then he danced it around, a frogman executing an involved slow-motion minuet, until a sudden current cut in and whirled the night-dress away, tumbling it beyond visibility, like a jiving partner too vigorously spun who wheels, arms flailing, right out of the room.

When Holmes was a boy suffering through history class – this was before Roger Christopher had entered the island school system like an exploding air embolism in the brain of a diver – the long litany of dates, of explorers and fur-trading routes, bored steadily into his head but failed to penetrate. The point of it all escaped him, likewise his nodding catatonic classmates. Dead is dead, so why dig it up? But when Holmes started diving, snorkelling at first, then drawn deeper and deeper into the lake, he made a surprising discovery: that the past has a pulse you can actually touch, that it can be disturbingly alive, a stranger speaking to you in the dark telling you the most incredible things. He discovered, too, that he had a flair for it, a creative receptivity, as well as a technical talent for assembling and fixing the hardware that hinged the past to the present.

He held up the blue medicine bottle and let it fill with light, as it had once been filled with Foo Choo's Balsam of Shark Oil. *Hear what the deaf say: It has performed a miracle in my ears.* Holmes ran his finger along the side seam of the bottle, following it up the neck and through the lip. That meant it was made sometime after 1903, though probably hadn't been tossed into the channel until after 1913, the year the railway bridge was completed.

Sitting in the control booth of the bridge, a cabin situated up in the lattice girders like a tree house built among iron branches, you could look down in 1913 and see the CPR train on her run from the mainland to the island, crossing on this iron hyphen from one word – and world – into another. The fireman, 'Horse Piss' Haines, might be recovering that day from a huge meal, Davy Warrior potatoes baked on top of the broiler near the safety valve, a huge steak fried on the coal shovel and taking a last swig of Foo Choo's for heartburn – *What the heck!* – flings the empty bottle into the channel as the train clatters over the bridge.

Truth lurked in these approximations to it, Holmes believed, the way treasures were hidden below the waterline, obscured by reeds and mud that the passing years thundering by like the train had conjured. He raised the medicine bottle to his lips and took a sip, an elixir of light that indeed might have sharpened his hearing, for beyond the sound of the phantom train whistle fading in the distance (the trains hadn't run in years), he heard boat horns blowing impatiently below. Then he remembered. He *was* in the control booth of the bridge, filling in for Austin Bates who was at his sister's wedding in the Sault. How about that. It must be time to pull the levers that swung the bridge slowly open, as Auz did on the hour without fail, letting through the high-masted sailboats and elaborate yachts that couldn't otherwise pass. The rest of the time Auz operated the lights at either end of the bridge, regulating car traffic on and off the island with an almost mechanical precision. You could rely on Auz, you could set your watch by him, but Holmes approached the job more intuitively, with an altogether more relaxed grip on time. You could even say that he was a man with time on his hands, a bountiful replenishing supply of it which he let slip easily and without regret through his fingers. He had trouble comprehending anxiety about lost seconds and minutes that were to him like petty cash, pennies you threw away on the street. Telling time was a confrontation with numbers he usually avoided – really, a quarter to *this*, and half past *that*, seemed a miserly apportioning of the whole pie. He didn't want to spend his life gazing into a clock face, as if into a mirror, watching in horror as the revolving razor-sharp hands shaved him to the bone. Funny how people physically tried to stop time. Wrestling it to the ground, clenched hard in their faces, and all they ever got for the effort was a more deeply engraved set of wrinkles. Like those vacationing yacht club sailors below who would soon be dead on their decks of heart attacks if he didn't open the bridge immediately. He wondered what kind of appointments they had with the gulls and the rocks on the other side of the channel to cause this seething urgency. Sometimes he liked to tease them by opening the bridge part way, then closing it again. He then would retrieve from his shirtfront pocket a dimestore telescope, the plastic one from the pirate set his young friend Rita Cabal had given him, and with it determine the degree of blood that rushed to their faces. A subtle art, like reading a thermometer through a keyhole. If you wanted more than a superficial purchase of time, was Holmes's opinion, then it was better to submerge yourself in it than to skim like this over its restless and mutable surface.

A man at the bottom of a lake is in no particular hurry. He has time to consider the drifting specks and motes that sift down carrying their cargo of reflected light, and to appreciate paddling loon feet and Stanfield-white duck bottoms, and to engage in a staring contest with a lawyer fish or think up lyrics for a lime green lip-synching bass. Absolved of gravity, allowed a taste of immortality, he can float through the water's blue expanse like a god in the sky. Holmes swam through days and weeks like this, through event, circumstance and weather, without feeling much compunction to measure it, except perhaps with this last object, the silver sundial. Ancestor to the pocket watch, it pricked the day with the finest of shadows, leaving a slight travelling bruise. When he held the sundial on his palm, life-lines buried beneath it, the time it told Holmes was long and continuous rather than brief and divided. And when he raised it up to the bright sunlight that poured through the window, he knew that he was holding something vital drawn out of a great depth. Finding the unexpected like this in the lake always gave him the startling sensation of reaching into the dark and grasping someone's hand, and of pulling them encrusted and forgotten and dead as Lazarus, into his warm receiving arms.

'Peter was having an affair!' Irene Inch had burst through the door, cartwheel hat askew and penis in hand, shaking it furiously at Innis, as though this were the sordid evidence torn off in a rage and turned to stone in her petrifying grip. She thumped it down hard on his cherry Art Nouveau glass-topped desk and a crack shot across the surface like a streak of lightning aimed directly at his heart. She dropped into one of his lucite shield-back chairs with the moulded bunting and trapezoidal upholstered seat and yanked open her purse, fat as a gut, from which Innis assumed she would withdraw a hanky to dab at her moist bewildered eyes. Or a little something at least to pay for the glass. Instead, she spat a half-sucked blackball smack into the depths of her purse and snapped it shut. 'I never suspected a *thing*.' Her lashing tongue was a pekingese purple. Irene had some peculiar habits.

'An affair? *Your* brother?' To which Innis could have added, the retiring and scholarly Dr Inch? The esteemed, world-renowned Mariologist? The aesthetic, soft-spoken, indeed hush-puppy-mouthed and ethereal, I'm-so-smart-my-feet-don't-even-touch-the-ground Dr Inch? That prim not to mention repressed pain in the ass was getting some nooky on the side? Unbelievable. 'Who with?'

'A vulva-puller.'

'I beg your pardon?'

'An anus-shower, a tongue-sticker, a foliage-spewer.'

'Ah, someone at the University.'

'An acrobatic megaphallic exhibitionist.'

'An engineer, then. I should have guessed.'

'The Romanesque, Innis. During all our research trips to Europe he was sneaking around on me, diddling with those hideous twelfth-century church carvings. Dallying in old religions. Fertility cults. He was slumming around with bog men. Do you know what I found when I started cleaning out his office? Boxes and boxes of papers, books, photographs, and *things*.' She eyed the offending artifact which stood pertly at attention between them. 'Nothing at all on Mary. *Not* a shred. I honestly had no idea Peter was so depraved, so academically ... promiscuous.'

'But, Irene. I mean, come on, this is silly. Naturally he'd have all kinds of interests outside of his area. Who knows, maybe he was bored with Virgin studies. He could have been suffering from some sort of intellectual midlife crisis and just needed to try out some new positions with some fresh material.'

'The pathetic fumbling gropings of a dirty old scholar? No, I think not. He was clearly obsessed, and it must have been going on for years under my very nose. Whenever I asked him about the book, our collaboration, he kept putting me off, saying he was still polishing the text, that it would be devastatingly brilliant when it was finished, and controversial – he'd mined a whole new vein of Virgin gold. Innis, the manuscript doesn't exist, I've searched everywhere for it. He never wrote a *word*.'

'Really?' Innis was beginning to enjoy himself.

'On his deathbed he kept repeating the same thing over and over, *luxuria, luxuria*, until that prurient light in his eyes flickered out, and his tongue went limp, and he died.'

'His very last words were in *Latin?*'

'Sins of the flesh, Innis. I thought he was raving.'

'But he was trying to tell you something. What about this stuff you found in his office?'

'Garbage. Shards and scraps. Nothing connects up.'

'Want me to examine it?'

'Would you?'

Would he? Was this not right up his alley? (Dark, dark.) Was this not in his line, no matter the line was broken into dashes for invisibility? Put your finger on exactly what it is he does, or what you think he does, and you'll be touching air. Iconologist? Investigative antiquarian? Doors opened magically for him, at Christie's, at Sotheby's, at the British Museum and the Louvre; portals sacred and tightly sealed, tiny and golden as those of tabernacles, surrendered to him their secrets. The tastefully designed shingle bearing his name – Innis C. George – that swung above *his* door, sun-scabbed and ivy-crowned, was like a stone under which writhed any number of occupational definitions that once revealed flashed away out of sight. His business card was blank as a ghost's. Never mind. Let him be furtive. Slipping in and out of skins not his own, a wardrobe of selves. Those who needed him managed to find him. He didn't have to advertise. Didn't have to strut around displaying his resplendent fan of talents, his unusual, if indefinable, gifts. Requests fell into his lap. And money. And occasionally, interesting objects.

Take it, Irene had said of the stone phallus. Innis protested, arguing its potential worth, but not too vehemently.

'You see,' Irene said, rooting around in her swag-bellied purse, 'you two deserve each other.'

Plumbing the depths of this comment was as likely for Innis as comprehending the contents of Irene's bulging black bag. Her medicine pouch, her bag of tricks, her *sac à main* fashioned out of fleshy material and adorned with a silver clasp and a bone handle. The mystery of women's purses. The rich noisy clatter they emitted, slack-jawed, as a hand scrabbled around inside ferreting out some exotic, elusive item. Watching Irene seize upon something with a triumphant smile, Innis felt a keen pang of purse envy. Not that he'd really want to be saddled with one himself. Didn't the great Dr Inch have a theory about purses, how women were compelled to lug them around like portable wombs, a ball-and-chain symbol of their biological burden? Maybe old Peter had more on his mind than the Virgin's holy handbag, after all.

Irene produced from her purse an obscenely large wad of pink pre-chewed gum, furry with lint, swaddled in tissue, which she then jammed into her mouth. Innis reached out, ran his finger lightly up the shaft of his new treasure, and shuddered.

On the drive north, distance rolling by like a film in which he was the leading man, Innis had plenty of time to muse, to sheath his stone sculpture in speculation, to let a brew of stimulating notions percolate through his head like strong black coffee. Pre-Christian, he thought, possibly even Iron Age, possibly Dionysian, the survivor of some frenzied possession cult. During the festival of the Phrygian Cybele young men castrated themselves and hurled their bleeding genitals out the window – it was considered good luck to catch one, like bridal candidates at a wedding lining up to catch the tossed bouquet. Phallic worship, no wonder it died out, at least in its more hysterical manifestations. His *did* occupy the dashboard like a vigorous icon, a pagan patron of the open road, an early saint of thrust and motion. How many pecks of pickled peckers did Peter Inch have? Innis had sorted through the clutter of Inch's eccentric collection, trying to find the thread that would tie it all together, or at least give it a credible drift. But it was all over the place, favouring no particular theme or time, consisting of odd narratives, maps, essays, fragments of poetry, amulets, fetishes, photographs, books written in tongues both living and dead. What was one to make of the Celts in bed with the Romans, hideous splay-legged *sheela-na-gigs* rubbing shoulders with classical statuary, an exquisite *bulla* – a necklace featuring a boyish member framed with cute ringlets of pubic hair – set against a massive stone penis on wheels that resembled a cannon? All he could really deduce from the evidence was that the stays that had held Inch's disciplined mind in place had loosened and that he had wandered off in thought, undone and wanton, into a red-light district of academe, subjective and literary.

Innis might have thrown in the towel altogether, declaring Inch's miscellany nothing more than the wreckage of an odd and perversely focused life, when a name caught his attention, a place name that kept bobbing to the surface in this welter of material. A suggestion even that something significant might be found there. Primary math, one plus one, added up to little more than a hunch, but enough of one for Innis to travel on. He'd gone on less before, driving a supposition home, no matter how convoluted the journey, and parking it smoothly in its most certain conclusion. He would do this, he decided. Easily. A quick sidetrip through his atlas had revealed this place to be surprisingly close at hand, and a few days sliced out of his week would scarcely leave a scar. His confidence in himself and in his uncanny sleuthing skills was as solid as the vehicle in which he presently travelled, trusty divining rod on the dashboard pointing the way.

Gazing at it, grey-skinned, pitted, caressed by time – it *was* handsome – Innis realized that he had grown extremely fond of the thing. Somehow it reminded him of that Dave Clark doll he'd once had, with the vinyl head and the inflatable hair, that he'd sold to a collector for a princely sum. But *this* was priceless. He imagined its long trajectory through history, stiff as a bat, true as an arrow, its ancient magic and power still intact. *What a piece of work is man*, he muttered to himself as he carried it into roadside restaurants with him, the better to observe it among its fellow objects, the ketchup bottles, water glasses, and other erect condiments and tableware. He was oblivious of the storm of trucker and waitress body language it evoked, the raised eyebrows, the smirks and sly smiles, the nudges and rude hand signs that ricocheted around him like a theatre performance confined to the rigours of mute and minute gesture. Continuing northward, he blazed a trail with it, through stands of spruce and cedar bush, past drumlin fields and moraines. He sliced through the limestone and shale-layered escarpment like a knife through a wedding cake. He was Gilles Villeneuve at the wheel, his Triumph devouring the road like a ravenous red beast. He cranked up the radio and he was Jerry Lee Lewis attacking the keyboard, thrusting this journey forward with evangelical zest and gusto.

In an excess of imagined stardom, he snatched the stone carving off the dashboard and howled into it. He was distracted … the heat, the frenzied applause, the sweat in his eyes … he couldn't see straight. He squealed around a sharp corner and failed to notice the sudden appearance of a bridge, the warning red light, the sudden *disappearance* of the bridge as it swung away from the land.

Say what?

From his vantage point in the control booth of the bridge, Holmes Stink watched as the small red car flipped off the road like a tiddly-wink, took a brief vertiginous spin in the air, then plunged into the channel. *Oh brother,* he thought.

Innis meanwhile, had opened his mouth to scream, but all that came out was *Great balls of fire!*

Nightwalkers

THE DEAD MAN'S boots were kept in the closet of the spare room. His shirts hung there, too, like skin on thin wire coat hangers. Fancy skin, with pearl buttons and fringes and embroidered roses blue as tattoos. Sometimes, late at night, the Dead Man put on his boots and one of his creepy satiny blood-red shirts and wandered through the house bumping into the furniture. (The Dead Man had no pants, or at least he couldn't find any.) Sometimes he stood outside Rita's door, breathing noisily, a laboured and rasping effort, even though Rita knew this was impossible because he was dead and empty and breath had ended in him, cut off like an unfinished sentence. Rita would lie in her bed, holding her own quick breath, playing possum, pretending to have nothing that he could possibly want, not a heartbeat, not a future, not a body like a tightly clasped purse containing a treasure trove of warmth and working parts worth their weight in gold. *How* to get rid of him? She imagined bright effacing light, prayer with needle-sharp piranha teeth, burning dissolving acid like the kind she wanted to splash in the eyes of the boy at school who ate erasers and left beaver dents in his pencils and even sucked his thumb and had the nerve to call *her* names. *Bug off, Sucker!* she said, the name that everyone called that snot-picking earwax-flicking kid, and the Dead Man stopped haunting her door with his gassy sulphurous breath, and walked away. Just like that.

Sofia Cabal called her daughter a night person, by which she meant, simply, that the child never seemed to sleep (except perhaps in school, Rita's forehead on her desk, and the other kids snickering around her like tapping leaves in her dream as Mr Christopher reaches out to drop something wet and amphibious down the back of her shirt). Though *night person* could be taken to mean more in Rita's case, describing something of her character, the material out of which she was cut, the dark cloth. She was like a figure in a Giorgione painting, but one who had stepped back into the black pigment, out of the luminous centre of the canvas. 'I heard you up walking around again last night,' Sofia said at breakfast. *That wasn't me,* Rita shrugged, shoving cornflakes into her mouth. *I don't bump into things.* Which was true. She could climb out of her window at night and negotiate the brickwork, the drainpipe, the trellis, noiselessly, sliding down the wall like a shadow. A dark knot of energy intent on some mission, most likely some harebrained initiation rite devised by the Snakes, the boys' club she so badly wanted to belong to. Ronny Evans was a kingsnake, and her friend Greg Lane a Massasauga rattler, and Rob Moonie, who was a bit on the tubby side, was a puff adder. 'When you join,' they laughed, 'you can be a *garter* snake because you're a girl.' A *dumb girl* this also implied, and in a few years make that *stupid pussy,* but not yet, all *that* was still latent. There, but not there. They knew the words and even the story but like alcohol it hadn't hit the bloodstream yet. And they knew of course that she wasn't dumb, or harmless, or constricted by odious pink-sashed girlhood, by the innumerable clips, snaps, and knobby garters that seemed to hold it all in place. She had done things they would never *dream* of doing, just to gain admittance to their club. She had walked in the graveyard at midnight on Hallowe'en, which, as any kid could tell you, was carnival night for the skeletons and half-rotted corpses. (*Wear your worms, your slime suits, your* joie de mort *perfume!*) This night of all nights, Abe Abatossaway throws back the trapdoor of earth over him and rises up, his soldier's uniform rumpled, decorated with medallions of blue mould, a hole in his chest where his heart used to be. Blake Hardy slaps himself together again like Osiris, like an amateur's poorly constructed quilt, and stumbles into town to pitch pebbles at Liz Stronghill's window as he used to do not so long ago. Jimmy Mann and his drowned dog Hoot leap up resuscitated, buoyed now on a wave of piss and vinegar, to *chase you,* dodging in and around the tombstones and out of your mind.

'Did you *see* them?' the boys asked, credulity conquering skepticism as they studied her face closely.

'I *saw* them,' Rita answered evenly, convincingly. 'I saw them all.'

In fact the only encounter she had was with old Gladdin Doan, who was very much alive, though an honorary citizen of the graveyard. 'I'm working the midnight shift,' he said to Rita, patting the grass on his son's grave as though it were a springing tuft of hair. Perlen Doan. A running leaping harum-scarum boy stilled below, a dark pucker on his temple like a kiss. Seventeen, always. People said the Stinks were involved but Rita didn't believe it, *they* got blamed for everything. Like that punch-up in the church. She'd been hiding behind the vestry door and had watched the whole manic choreography of the moment, a swift reeling fandango of fists, elbows and knees (Father Finn's nose crossing the sea of his cheek like a sail), until a thick curtain of smoke dropped from the ceiling and obscured her view. 'My Perly feels the wind,' Gladdin told her. 'He feels it moving in the earth the way it moves through a field of wheat.' *Mad Glad*, some said, for having walked the long leaf-canopied aisle to this stone altar like a bride with a groom, turning his back on the town and the living. He had set up housekeeping in the surrounding woods, in a shack with muskrat tails for curtains (they also said), where he ate off a place setting of soup and sardine cans and kept company with a pet fox. Visitors to the cemetery brought him baskets of food, bottles of milk, black bass or pike wrapped in newspaper, and placed these offerings at the foot of Perlen's grave. In gratitude or kindness, honouring old debts. Gladdin had been a doctor and the island coroner, but had buried that practice with Perlen, his only son and last client. 'I've diagnosed this kind of paralysis before,' he said, stroking the grave, and the raw love that poured out of him so freely, a man haemorrhaging emotion, scared Rita even more than a real ghost might have done, and she took off for home. She *ran* and *ran* and the November cold reached up through the ground, up through her thin-soled shoes to rake at her back.

Oh, they all came out of the woodwork at night. The insomniacs, the dog-walkers, the worm-pickers, the sprightly firefly enthusiasts and the bat-eared moth-lovers. Those who muttered poetry or cursed quietly to themselves, or confronted invisible antagonists, telling them off in high style – *touché!* Those who soliloquized in the bushes, those who whistled. Those who strode silently by bearing a brimful burden of words in their heads and never spilling a one. And then there were the *others*. The night creatures who walked, brazen and boldfaced, directly out of myth and make-believe, as if what separated fact from fiction was not an impenetrable wall, but a flimsy beaded curtain easily swept aside.

Rita's hair bristled. She was aware of a presence near her bed, most likely her guardian angel. Unlike the Dead Man, her guardian angel had a passport to her room signed by the Pope himself, and he would appear unpredictably and stand staring at her, golden eyes

alight. To Rita he was more like a menacing older brother than a pro-
tective spirit. His breath smelled of cloves and he was always fastidiously dressed, but she suspected him of vile, undisclosed habits, and
he was unreliable.

Dear God, Rita prayed, *I don't mean to complain, and I know you're
busy, but I think you should speak to Chamuel. I'm almost sure he's been
shitting on the roof behind the chimney. Really, they're big. And they keep
rolling off, the wind blows them. The other day one landed in the brim of
Mrs Fletcher's hat. You know her, she's president of the Ladies' Auxiliary,
and mother was so embarrassed.*

Father Finn explained to Rita that angels don't have human func-
tions and that one mustn't confuse celestial beings with earthly ones.

In the church basement workshop – his clinic for fractured saints
and other maimed statuary – Victor Cabal overheard his daughter
pestering the priest with her irreverent nonsense. He shook his head
sadly. Faith was such a fragile vessel and he feared that Rita would
never learn to carry it carefully enough, respectfully enough. Faith
was not going to survive her eager, fumbling grasp of it. 'Do nuns
wear black underwear?' she asked Father Finn. And, 'What if that
cloth Jesus wears fell off during mass? Would that be a miracle, or
more like the bad thing Stu Stink did in front of the grade one class?'
Meu Deus. Would he have *ever* dreamed as a boy of asking such questions of the village priest, a man so stern and godlike Victor had
hardly been able to squeak out a confession to him. But priests, kids.
They'd all come down in the world. '*Your* fault,' he accused Saint
Clair, who was in for a nose job and a fresh coat of paint. As the
patron saint of television, *she* was responsible for that baneful mind-
vacuuming invention. 'Satan watches TV,' he told her, 'and we're the
show.'

Later, Victor apologized to the priest. 'Rita has this imagination,'
he said, making it sound like a mortal sin. 'Too much. And ever since
her uncle died, it's gotten worse. She hears things, sees things.'

Father Finn absolved her easily with a laugh. 'C'mon, Vic, don't
worry. Rita's curious, it's only normal. Besides, she probably *is* hearing things. I'll bet you five bucks you've got raccoons in your chimney. Better set a few traps.'

'Hmph.' Victor stared at him, God's mediator, and thought how
much the priest himself resembled a raccoon, a masked Lone Ranger
of the night, with those two black eyes, a matched set that had come

with his recently acquired boxer's nose. He wondered if Saint Clair would like one in that style. A change from the usual nasal pimple that passed for a nose in ecclesiastical statuary. These icons were as bad as movie stars with their nips and tucks.

'Hey, Father,' he held up a Roman nose in his palm. A real beaut. 'What do you think? Would you pick it?'

Irreverence, after all, was as contagious as the common cold.

Rita hated to admit it, but she was related to the Dead Man. The blood scent of their affiliation drew him, and she wanted to sever it like an artery. While alive the Dead Man had existed for her mainly in the safety of words. In heated family discussions he rode the turbulence like a stuntman. 'Got a card from that no-good brother of yours,' Sofia might say with a provocative smile, and set Victor off, cursing and fuming. Rita usually heard her uncle defined in terms that seemed primarily reptilian, like some creature she might study in school. *The Goddamn Portuguese Lounge Lizard. Habitat: smoky bars. Food: raw steak. Mating Practices: predatory and voracious.* On a couple of occasions her uncle actually stepped out of the angry swirl of words and appeared in person. He dazzled Rita then with his slick looks and smooth entertainer's patter and his armful of extravagant presents. And he didn't insult her, either, by bringing her dolls, although he confessed with a wink that he liked to play with them himself. She admired his honesty about that and she liked his energetic attack, how he stirred up the torpid atmosphere of the house like an electrical storm striking with bad jokes, or salty lounge lyrics, or crackpot get-rich-quick schemes advanced mainly to aggravate her careful, abstemious father. His departures were unexpected, and abrupt, as if he had simply vanished. Rita would burst into the house, home from school, to find her mother locked in the bathroom crying, and her father enclosed in an unbreachable silence – no words, no uncle.

Death had ruined him for Rita. It had thickened him, rendered him clumsy and earnest, numb as the furniture he stumbled into. Sofia had made Rita touch him – she had been strangely insistent. He had arrived at their door one last time, grey-faced and empty-handed, and couldn't be turned away. At that point, their door and death's door must have been indistinguishable to him. So Rita touched him, not expecting the warmth she felt, in life his hands had always been so dry and cool. Shocked, she drew away, but it was too late. His touch stuck to her unshakably like a stretchy string of gum, connecting them, bringing him at night unwanted and needy and terrible to her bedroom door, the dead weight at the other end of the idiot mitten.

To Rita their house seemed cursed, stained, marked with an x – why else would something incredibly large be shitting on their roof? Her mother was forever sniffling and coughing because the furnace, that multi-armed monster in the basement, tossed facefuls of dust through the registers like a malicious witch at a wedding. Grey, leprous mould grew on the walls, and cupboard doors came right off their hinges in your hands, as though you'd suddenly developed brute strength. Rita much preferred to spend her spare time at the church, where her father worked as caretaker and cosmetician for its plaster population.

She loved to watch him work, painting eyes, lips, the sky-blue hem of Mary's cloak, the beef-bright red of the Sacred Heart, the colour so perfect he might have dipped the brush in his own blood. Victor had learned his trade in Lisbon and carried it here to this Canadian island, a cathedral of limestone and pine. *Fool*, his family had said, envisioning newsreels of him buried in snow, scalped, and eaten alive by beavers, and not a Mountie in sight. But his move, the giant step he took across the ocean, turned out to be something of an occupational coup, for the country was not exactly overrun with religious artisans. More and more now, Father Finn did the sweeping up while Victor doctored the chipped and broken statues that came for repair from all over the diocese. And since his patients often arrived in the company of other more prosaic deliveries to the island, you never knew who or what might appear: Saint Catherine say, in a Cecutti's Bakery truck, reclining like an odalisque on a cushiony fragrant ottoman of Wonder bread, or Saint Francis stone-cold and orphaned on the church steps after roistering these many northern miles with a cargo of frozen turkeys.

Among the saints her father was at his best, Rita decided. He was so funny, teasing and scolding them, and not just for her benefit, knowing she was listening and delighted by it. They were his buddies, his confidants, *his* gang, and he was their leader. 'You should be ashamed of yourself,' he shook his finger at Saint Anthony, patron of lost things.

'*You*, losing your halo like that. I had to get down on my hands and knees and crawl around like a crab looking for it.' Sometimes he got carried away and called them *cement heads* and threatened to have them demoted like Saint Christopher, but there were boundaries he honoured, lines of respect that he just didn't cross.

Once when Rita was stretched out on one of the pews doing homework after school, her father came upstairs with her uncle to show him the crucifix above the altar, some tricky detailed work he'd done on it. Her uncle was impressed, but more with the figure of Christ, which was so well proportioned and lifelike. A suffering Christ, true, but one that was almost romantically handsome, with fine sculpted legs and a strong body, not like some you see, chicken-thin and yellowish, an unappealing stylized ugliness.

'Oh *man*,' her uncle said. 'He looks so real. You can almost see Him climbing down off that thing at night, eh? Yeah, walking around, looking things over. Maybe sits at the back with his legs crossed, having a smoke. Thinking, you know. Doesn't even notice but He's poking a finger through His palm, sorta like Marlon Brando in that movie where he puts on the girl's white glove. Yeah. He's thinking about that pretty little nun who sits in the front row, how He'd like to give her a few visions, eh, a little ecstasy on a Saturday night. Stigmata? Sweetheart, listen, He'd tell her, I can make you really bleed.'

'*Cale-se!*' her father said. 'You filthy bastard,' and he walked away, disgusted.

Another time, when Rita was sitting on the couch at home beside her uncle, she asked him about snakes – he used to know a few things before his brain cells collapsed like a pile of ashes, before he got to be so dead and stupid. 'Uncle, what is the baddest snake?'

'The baddest? You mean like a real killer? Let's see, the bushmaster, he's a bad one, don't mess with him. The boomslang, the Australian taipan, both mean mothers. The spitting cobra, he'll blind you, spit venom right in your eyes. Wait, I *know*. Yeah.' Her uncle smiled that slow satisfied rat-eating smile of his, and said, 'The *black mamba*. That's him. He's the deadliest, and he strikes fast. Like *this*.'

And he shot his hand up her bare leg under her dress and fingered her crotch, a swift licking stroke that sent a wild ticklish thrill jabbing up into her body before she could even think to say, *Yes. That's the one I want to be.*

Various Delusions

SISTER ST. ANNE LOST her soul. It beat its way out of her and escaped through an open window, the umbilical cord of it paying out of her solar plexus like a long unwinding entrail of light. *That* dream. She had been wandering the corridors of the hospital, checking room after room – all empty, bedpans stacked, sheets neatly and precisely tucked, everything so white that whiteness bled into blue. Very strange. Where had everyone gone? Only yesterday the place was packed, stretchers lined up in the hall. She pushed open the door of Room 301, old Mrs Stink's room, the burn patient, and was surprised to find instead a visitor, a *holy* visitor, a divine manifestation, call him Saint x (she was loath to name him, even in her dream). He was kneeling on the bed, a twisted body of sheets lapping against him. He was kneeling though not praying, no, he was abusing himself, quite cheerfully, gleefully even. 'Look out,' he shouted, and a phenomenal cambered stream of semen smacked onto the front of her habit and rained down into her hands like a shower of gold. Amazement woke her, and it was then that her soul leapt out of her like an instant improvisational birth and fled. She raised her hands to her face and smelled them. A rank odour. Like old pennies, like dead trout. Like sin.

Walking down the congested hospital corridor later in the day, Sister St. Anne kept her hands turned shamefully in, hidden in the black folds of her habit. As three nurses whirled past – a new patient had been rushed in, dragged half-drowned out of the channel – she concentrated with a drunk's exaggerated effort on walking in a straight line. Without a soul her body tended to list into the walls. She felt incredibly heavy and wondered if souls didn't also serve some practical purpose like those air bladders fish have to keep them from sinking to the bottom. Was this a blasphemous notion? She might have to confess it along with her erotic dream, which hardly seemed fair considering her late arrival on the scene and the mess. Sister St. Anne was a clever mimic and it crossed her mind that she might borrow Sister Bernadette's voice for the confessional, Father Finn would never guess. Sister Bernadette was so pious it was sickening and a few debits in her spiritual account book wouldn't hurt.

On the whole it might improve her credibility. She was well named, that one, as St. Bernadette was said to have been a dim-witted girl with asthma and a limited imagination.

For all the difficulty she was having, Sister St. Anne might have been a river-walker pushing her way upstream, opposing the current, her legs flaring out, oddly refracted. She stumbled and veered dangerously close to a portrait of the Pope, nearly sending it flying off the wall. When Dr Nopper hove into view travelling at a great clip, this is how things stood with her: her soul had cut loose and was sailing free over the town. Her hands tingled. A pungent odour crept out of the shadowy folds of her habit, and bad intentions multiplied in her head with a reproductive ferocity, compounding interest like microbes in a Petri dish.

Dr Nopper's apologies fluttered down like finches and perched on her chest where they cocked their quick golden heads and stared at her quizzically. On the other hand, Dr Nopper was thinking to himself, *neurotic nun, what's gotten into her?* He had been about to pass her in the hall when she had inexplicably lurched in front of him and he flattened her, laid her out on the hospital floor like a stretch of black-and-white linoleum. 'Oh … *heavens*,' he said, grasping her hands to help her up. Her weight surprised him, he had expected a layered lightness. 'My fault entirely. Please forgive me, Sister Bernadette (they all looked the same to him). Are you all right?' Sister St. Anne cursed a blue stream of invective under her breath, accumulating further confessional matter, and turned to wander back down the hall. Dr Nopper scratched his chin thoughtfully as he watched her go, watched her walk as though she were stitching one wall to another with invisible thread. His fingers he then noticed were stained with a peculiar sticky substance, earthy smelling, like mulch or decay, and he wondered, *What in God's name is that?*

Possibly a new epidemic was brewing, one of those oddball ones like bongo drum disease or flip-flop dermatitis, this one peculiar to nuns. Wimple fatigue. Bride of Christ syndrome. Celibitis. The creative range and industry of bacteria never failed to thrill Dr Nopper. Really and truly, a healthy person was seventy percent water and the rest illusion, he simply didn't exist. After years of practising medicine, he had come to the conclusion that everyone has something wrong with them, and if they don't they *think* they do, which is just as bad. Once a man came into his office complaining of lumps growing on the side of his feet and had asked nervously if Dr Nopper thought they were benign. *Yes*, he answered, after examining the man, *of course they're benign, they're your ankles.* Another patient of his had taken to operating on herself, surgical self-improvement to accompany the home perm. She had given herself a chin-tuck, shortened her toes and removed her earlobes, which drooped she said. It seemed that symptoms and pathologies were limited solely by their victims' imaginative reach. And every last thing named in the world had a dark side, a phobia that shadowed it, and some blessed fool terrified of it. There were people who were frightened to death of pins. *Pins!* And *flutes* and *skin* and *rivers* and even *rectums.* Rectophobia it was called. And onomatophobia, fear of *names.* And fear of *words*, logophobia. And even *this* might do you in, he thought, plucking a long-stemmed rose out of an abandoned arrangement at the nurse's station, if flowers happened to be the thing that gave your fear form.

Brandishing the rose like a hot poker, he swashbuckled into Room 301, which caused the RNs who were gathered like Fates around the new patient to exclaim in chorus, 'Oh doctor, he's lost his penis!'

'Of course he has. Am I surprised? Man's greatest fear, isn't it? Except for Tchaikovsky. He was afraid his head was going to fall off. Let me have a look.'

He handed the flower to Sue-Ellen Smart, who made a face – 'Ew' and tossed it in the garbage. 'It stinks.' She hated roses anyway, they turned her stomach. They were too fleshy somehow, obscene, like blood clots on sticks. They were vegetable exaggerations, the big romantic statement, the great floral cliché. Women got them for everything, for having babies, for anniversaries, for dying even. And in her mother's case, for each bruise sustained on a drunken Saturday night. For each whorled blue flower her father placed on her mother's skin. And in the morning, in his arms the *red* ones. For forgiveness. For getting royally fucked.

'You don't have to frown, Sue-Ellen,' said Dr Nopper, 'it's not *that* small.' He tossed back the covering sheet. 'As you can see, ladies and germs, the honourable member is present and accounted for. Though I can certainly understand how you all overlooked it.'

'Oh, we didn't really think he'd *lost* it,' said Mimi Wolinski. 'It's just that he's been going on and on about it, he's delirious.'

'Ah.' Dr Nopper reached to take his patient's pulse at the very moment that Innis George felt a woman's hand, fingers worn and hard, touch his wrist. In the dark he couldn't see what she was like, whether young or old, beautiful or eroded. He only knew it was a woman with a rough hand leading him forward while all the fish in the water he'd swallowed leapt like quicksilver in his veins. He was on a pilgrimage, he knew that too. This was the secret underwater passage. He had lost the carving. Gone, gone. He searched and searched for it, but found only a book that had spiralled up past his face while a current riffled madly through the pages, back and forth, like someone desperate to relocate a memorable phrase. The woman had a fierce unrelenting grip. *Wake up*, she whispered, her voice raven-throated like the waves on the shore sucking gravel. Something black came out of his mouth. His arms glowed, the water elfed his hair into knots. He gazed up toward the surface and saw three gorgons and a satyr staring down at him. He wanted to show them his companion – *Look what I found!* – but the woman's hand snapped off, wooden and worm-eaten, the rest of her tumbling away. Her jagged thumb left a hole in his wrist through which the most astonishing green blood began to flow. It spilled out of his wrist and into his face like a tipped bottle of perfume with an otherworldly bouquet, a scent heavenly as crushed roses. Innis kicked his feet and swam up a level or two toward light and consciousness. He smiled in his sleep.

'*See*. He's going to snap out of it. Pulse is racing a bit, but he'll survive. He's had quite a shock, you know. Now,' Dr Nopper turned to the other patient in the room, 'how's Granny today?'

'Piss off,' she said.

'She's sulking. Mr George has been getting all the attention.' LaBelle Stink cocked open a crusty green eye. 'I lost a tit in '59 and you never heard me carryin' on like that.'

Dr Nopper grazed her forehead with his fingers and gently prized her jaws open to slide a thermometer under her sharp tongue.

LaBelle snapped her eye shut and climbed back down to the root cellar where she was gathering sweetings out of a basket. She pressed them to her cheeks, fragrant and cool, round as breasts in her hands, then filled her apron and dashed up the stairs, her long braid whapping against her backbone, heavy as a snake. Mother was making apple dumplings, date pies, bilberry tarts and pans of cinnamon buns, the kitchen becoming so dense with the intoxicating aroma of spices and baked fruit in pastry that LaBelle thinks she has died and gone to heaven. From this point in time, how could she ever guess that she would live to see herself cooked like a dessert by her own progeny, the burnt-sugar stench of her own flesh seeping into her brain, poking vents in her memory, making her mother glance up from a mixing bowl bulging with a rump-thick batter and say, sniffing suspiciously, *Who cut the cheese?*

'Which reminds me,' Dr Nopper scribbled a few hieroglyphics on LaBelle's chart, 'did any of you read the piece in the paper this morning about that new archaeological discovery?'

'We had to be into work by *six*.'

'No? Fascinating. Three pairs of ancient human breasts were found at the bottom of a lake in Germany.'

'Gross.'

'They were made of clay, but life-size. And *six thousand* years old.'

'Lord. No wonder they were at the bottom of the lake. Mine are halfway to my knees already and I'm only thirty.'

'Haw!'

'Say Mimi, did your ever find that missing cat of yours ...'

LaBelle Stink was wearing a cloak of bees, gloves encrusted with the furry topaz bodies of bees, and a woven animate aureole of bees encircled her head. This at least was how she translated the conversation, the persistent droning hum that surrounded her, the tickling irritating words that crawled over her, up her nostrils and in her mouth, until finally, mercifully, they gathered up into a clamorous swarm, a dark floating veil of sound that began to recede, drifting into thin dissonant tatters, and then ... silence.

The room was empty. The two patients slept on, involved in their individual underworld activities. A fly buzzed through an open window, did a double flip and landed on the ceiling. Instantly its attention was drawn (its multi-faceted eyes goggling) to the aromatic mirage shimmering on Granny Stink's brow. It zoomed down and executed a two-point landing on her head, where it bounced around in ecstasy, performing lazy eights and barrel rolls, hedgehopping and taxiing up and down the spongy corrugated runway.

Of course the first thing Ruthie Stink saw when she walked into the room was the fly – Stink cohabitation had whetted her eye for vermin detection of this sort. She picked up a newspaper, rolled it tight as a log, and whapped Granny smartly in the face, smearing the fly across a front page picture spread of some guy holding a pair of stone breasts, one in each hand and looking hugely pleased with himself as he pointed them toward the camera.

Granny Stink's eyes flew open, both this time. 'You get that bee?'

'Yup. Bugger's jam now.'

'Good.' She chewed on that word for some time as though it had notable substance, as though it actually tasted of its own meaning. 'How's your mother?'

'I dunno.' Ruthie looked away, pursed her lips. The old bag knew damn well she and her mother weren't speaking. Let her rot.

'Oh, *please*, let me, just this once.'

'Who's the whiner?' Ruthie studied the new patient for a moment. 'Say, what's *he* doing in your room? This place go co-ed or something?'

'Lost his dink. Guess they figure he can't do no harm.'

'He *what*?' Ruthie laughed.

'Had it in his hand when he was drivin'. Musta snapped off.'

'Tsk, tsk. That's Tennessee Ernie's specialty. They'd make a good pair. Does he do magic tricks?'

'Nah. Alls he does is yap.'

Ruthie's interest was piqued and she wandered over to Innis' bed to have a closer look. Although he was drifting several fathoms below, and engaged in conversation with an oddly seductive carp (did this make him an ichthyophile, he wondered), he nonetheless drove his arm up through the deep water of his dream, and like an eel making a sudden strike, he socked his hand onto Ruthie's, his fingers biting hard into her skin. 'You are a *vision*,' he hissed. 'The most beautiful creature I've ever seen.'

'That's funny,' commented LaBelle. 'His eyes are closed.'

'Let go!' Ruthie yanked her hand away and retreated to the window. '*Geez.* That guy's lost more than his dink.' She rubbed her hand soothingly, protectively, trying to erase the impression left by his sweaty smarting grip. 'Geez,' she said again, staring out, looking directly through her own head reflected in the window glass. Her scrutiny of the air fell three stories and into the parking lot where she watched Sofia Cabal, the hospital's head cook, climb out of an old finned heap of a car. She watched as Sofia casually tossed her skirt up around her waist to hike up her pantyhose. She then lumbered toward the building, the back half of her skirt still rucked up and caught in her waistband. Hadn't Ruthie heard some strange rumour about that woman lately? Her gaze shot sideways and intercepted Roger Christopher, who was gliding up the street wearing – *come on, not really* – a wedding gown, and carrying a burlap sack big as a belly slung over his shoulder. *Another certified lunatic.* She raised her hand to wave, but the teacher had already coasted out of the picture, all but the crinolined hem of his dress which swished stiffly around a corner, and was gone.

Ruthie sniffed curiously at her fingertips, scrunching them into a nosegay of pink fleshy rosebuds, and smiled. Such a fond familiar smell. It reminded her of when she was a little girl, in grade two, and had asked one of the nuns – a Sister St. *X*, what *was* her name, she vanished shortly afterward – she asked her what sin smelled like. And the nun replied, 'Why, it smells like *semen*, dear.' And naturally Ruthie thought she meant the men who worked on the water, who smelled of fish and oil and sweat, or the mermen who lived in it and who smelled fresh and clean as apples, and she decided that she loved all those smells, she *loved* the smell of sin.

Her gaze rose up again like heat and caressed the sides of houses. It rubbed against brick, skimmed over rooftops, dodged around chimneys, until it encountered something flashing and bobbing in the distance that it couldn't honestly identify. What *was* it? Not a kite, or a snagged balloon. But winged and dazzling. Nothing, she felt, that human hands could ever make, or touch. Brilliant. So painfully bright in fact that Ruthie had to shield her eyes against it, closing them quickly, saying softly to herself, *Aaa-men.*

Creep

SNAKE SPILL. A writhing lightning-streaked waterfall splashing out of the dumped sack, tumbling over the desk, river as acrobat, breaking into a hundred weaving tributaries, flowing under children's leaping retracting feet, seeking the dark, seeking the pools and cavities of the underworld, wherever they might be found here in this ordinary classroom. Where? In a beckoning unstrapped Stewart plaid school bag, in a prostrate rubber boot flung by the door, in a chalet hideout a fallen reader makes, in a deep welcoming pocket furnished in high reptilian style with pebbles and moss and coiled string. Ectotherm meets endotherm, the matchmaker dressed to kill, but like many of Roger Christopher's lessons, it's not exactly love at first sight. Martha Wolinski, already traumatized by the loss of her cat Fluffy, and the loss of Noir before that, *screams* and *screams* making thousands of delicate snake bones vibrate like tuning forks, informing the stricken creatures that what they already knew instinctively about humankind is most certainly and horribly true. Several abrade their faces on rough walls in sharp corners trying to find a way out of this shuddering cacophonous tomb.

There *is* no way out, thinks Rita Cabal. What goes on in the classroom is private, a cocoon-soft straitjacket their teacher spins around them, no metamorphosis intended.

Greg Lane wiggles his eyebrows up and down at her, meaning, *What's with the dress?*

Rita shrugs, *Who knows.* Was there a naked blue bride stranded on the highway somewhere? Mr Christopher could charm the skin off a rat.

Today, apparently, they are studying a physical principle called 'creep', a poem by D.H. Lawrence, and a species of legless, elongated reptiles forming the suborder *Serpentes* of the order *Squamata*. The dress may have everything or nothing to do with all or none of the above. The lesson begins in the middle, a belly dance of words, a mesmerizing sinuous advance against which they are powerless. At some point he'll probably switch languages on them, sliding from a circuitous consonant-strewn path, familiar at least, into a flowing alien tongue, each vowel a glittering grasping scale. And they would not bat an eyelid, not even the two Stinks in the room. Stu Stink because he was impervious to instruction – facts swept past his ears and got sucked like dinner into the ever-open cave of his mouth – and Dinky Stink because he was sly. Dinky had to be almost fifteen and drove his own car to school, though he could barely see over the steering wheel, sometimes he sat on a rock. He was biding his time in grade school, waiting to grow. Once that was accomplished he would take a crowbar to this junior league he was stalled in and make a jailbreak. In the meantime he smoked half a pack at recess and sold the butts. You could also buy bootleg candy from him, blackballs and jelly babies, hooked from the variety store, as well as swigs from his silver flask, which contained either warm beer or Canadian Club. In class he watched Roger Christopher carefully, not betraying the slightest interest in anything the teacher said. Though Dinky liked his dress. He had a soft spot for lace.

If the children knew the word 'subversive', they could use it. It might just apply to a teacher who had rendered 'In Flanders Fields' into semaphore, or who had replaced their morning prayer, the 'Pater Noster' with something called the 'Gnat-Psalm'. Obviously the knowledge they needed, or thought they needed, wasn't forthcoming. Subversive? Let them look it up.

Rita felt something encircling her ankle, creating a tickling sensation like feathers sprouting, and glancing down saw the tail end of one of the snakes loosed from the sack vanish into her Annie Oakley lunch box. Earlier she had been poking around in it, searching for some tempting item to trade with Stu Stink – her homemade roll or slice of fig pie for his Cheeze Whiz on Wonder bread no wrapper. They found each other's food weird but useful. With a Cheeze Whiz locked in her hand at lunch like a six-shooter, she knew Sucker Lewis would have to think twice about calling her Dago or Spanish Onion, not that she wasn't born in this country same as him. Not on the island, though, and that marked you, sure as the stripes on this little snake. Rita reached down and snapped her lunch box shut, planning to release it out back after school, when she caught Dinky Stink's cool eye appraising her. The other girls said Dinky undressed you with his eyes, but Rita understood it to be a more surgical scrutiny than that, a gutting and filleting, a deft folding back of skin and muscle, a calculated fingering of the blood-sodden secrets within. When the lunch bell rang at noon, Dinky was gone, peeling off in his car to the pool hall, skunk tail swaying below the mirror, purple sex lights in the corner of the windshield winking off and on as he hit the potholes. In the morning when he slid like a shark into the space beside the principal's muskrat-brown sedan, kids gathered around to peer into his car's dark enticing interior. With its ornate clutter, dashboard statuary, fringed velvety upholstery and smoky incense-thick air, it reminded Rita of a church, a chapel on wheels. Though intended for what kind of worship she couldn't imagine. Or refused to. Just as she refused to be unnerved by his skin-stripping face-raking stare. He'd better watch it. Her eyes could shape and deliver a look as lethal as any he could devise. *You got Indian hair*, was the one and only thing Dinky had ever said to her, his hair exactly the same earth-black shade as hers, only slick with grease. 'It flows down the roof,' Roger Christopher was saying, determined to pull the rug out from under their stubbornly planted feet. 'Lead will seep *slowly* down a church roof. Stone lintels will sag. In time, even glass flows like water.' Rita could feel Dinky's eyes crawling up the back of her neck, a knifepoint slide up the sloppy staggering part her mother had made hurriedly braiding her hair. Her mother braided badly, the part like a ragged tear in Rita's head, a shamefully exposed cleft.

'It's effected largely through gravitational pull, dislocation, and rheologic deformation.'

Right, Rita thought, so when do I get to colour a bunny or something, glue macaroni onto a paper plate and paint it for Mother's Day?

'Him speak with forked tongue,' Greg muttered behind the shield of his hand.

Roger Christopher's tongue *was* like a fork that jabbed randomly at raw chunks of knowledge, holding them out for everyone to slaver over (hardly), then devouring them himself. He was devious, two-faced as the Jack of Spades, but Rita was wise to his tricks, this sleight-of-hand that would transform stone and metal, solid and reliable materials, into substances as shifting and unstable as the lake itself. He couldn't open his mouth without weaving together with his forked tongue truth and lies into a long tortuous braid. And it didn't seem to matter, either, what they extracted from it, what they unpicked from the weave. *A conservative*, Ronny Evans had written in answer to a question on a test, *is a sort of greenhouse where you go and look at the moon*, and for this he had received full marks and a gold star. Like a slick and accomplished Tennessee Ernie (whose magic snagged in his sleeves), Roger Christopher pulled incredible notions out of the air and presented them as fact. Snakes that can fly, lizards that squirt blood from their eyes or that shatter like glass and then regenerate, iguanas that spend their days nodding to one another and doing push-ups, worms that can creep forward as well as backward, fish that in the perverse course of their lives change from female to male. (Did he say *sex*?) He never discussed the safely fantastic, the witches or ghouls that knew their invented place, only the incredible inbred with the actual. (A male garter snake has *two*? Come on!) As children, it was their job to be steeped in awe, sugar-dusted in enchantments, bobbing up to their jaws in make-believe, but somehow Roger Christopher's lessons always left them feeling bankrupt and insufficient, as though the world were both more *and* less real than they could ever imagine.

You had to wonder what kind of Catholic he was, what kind of mongrel breed. He assailed them with the impossible, and yet scorned the miraculous. *Who paid for the Last Supper?* he asked one day in catechism class. Dead silence. *Jesus got nailed for it.* An old joke, but aired in the classroom sounding so brazen and fresh that it provoked laughter of the venial, mortal, and straight-to-hell varieties. Ronny crashed out of his seat like Satan hitting the floor. Roger Christopher could have lost his job over that one, something he risked daily anyway performing his highwire stunts on the ever-thinning patience of his employers. Not that the school board had much choice in teachers. Who but the educational dregs and misfits, elsewhere unemployable, would willingly work in these northern boonies, home of mouth-breathers and Stinks? The net was cast wide and the specimens dredged up were usually as odd as those finned creatures, the spook fish and gulper eels, they had watched rise like spectres out of the depths of Roger Christopher's lessons to float terrible in mid-phrase before them.

Rita's very first teacher in grade one was an ex-missionary who had greenish-grey hair and Mikado-yellow teeth. She managed to pass on to her young charges some basics in martial arts before being replaced by a business practice teacher from Orillia who experienced a spectacular nervous breakdown during math class when his head jammed like a malfunctioning adding machine. By Christmas Rita could separate a boy from his breakfast with a smartly executed kick and she could take dictation, but she couldn't write her own name to save her soul. A combination of shorthand and karate made quick work of her exercise books – *chop, chop* – toppling over neat rows of letters like dominoes, dismembering others, floating hair-thin limbs and serifs and stray dots in an unruly and animate paper air. Second term brought them a retired hairdresser, who was fun, but scandalized the parents by giving everyone beehives and mohawks, with not a single one of the three r's buzzing or burring in the heads they graced. She was followed by an Irish seminarian who spoke with such reverence and at such length about his mother, a woman named Mary Murphy, that Rita got her mixed up with the other Mary and thought it was the Virgin who'd had ten children – not counting the idiot – and who made the best blood pudding this side of Armagh. (Had Rita not heard Father Finn himself in passionate supplication of *Jesus Murphy?*)

Roger Christopher's instructional specialty was much harder to define. He skipped unpredictably from subject to subject, his curriculum protean and diffuse, at times as impossible to grasp as mercury. Whatever they had managed to scavenge and hoard in the way of education up to this point now seemed useless. He discarded what they knew, same as he dumped that sack of snakes on his desk. He wanted to see their mind's spawn in its writhing seething form, not dead and collected in a box. *Life*, he assured them, *breeds even on the fetid stinking tongue of a dead man.* Holy! Rita pictured Perly Doan speaking directly into the earth, speech feeding into the roots of grass, bursting out of the ground, spreading like green fire. *Ora boles*, as her father would say. *Nuts. Baloney.* Divine intervention Rita accepted. A statue of the Virgin trembling or weeping blood, people had *witnessed* such miracles. But who had ever seen stone or metal move of its own accord? Words rattled and spilled out of Roger Christopher's mouth like dice – snake eyes! Don't trust him. He turned the sacred acts of the saints and martyrs into antics, presenting them to the class as crackpot entertainment. Visceral slapstick, pratfalls out of the sky. St. Gerard Majella clocking in at half a mile of ecstatic flight, St. Wilgefortis growing a beard overnight to discourage a prospective husband, St. Lucy plucking out her eyes and delivering them to a lascivious suitor on a plate (one eye winking). His favourites, though, were Cosmas and Damian, the saintly doctors who transplanted a black man's leg onto the body of a sleeping white man who then awoke to find he had a pair of mismatched legs. A mirthful tear slid down Roger Christopher's cheek. What a saucy bride, sproinging red chest hair coiling out of his décolletage, a sceptical gleam infusing his eye. He infested Rita's beliefs, ate them from the inside out like a worm destroying an apple. Where was Chamuel, her coyly invisible guardian angel, when she needed him? Down at the pool hall watching Grace Stronghill sinking pockets while her gilded hair flashed like pieces of eight in the dim smoky room.

Two notes arrived air mail on Rita's desk. One a clean white jet of paper, the other crumpled into a soiled ink-smudged ball. She opened the jet first, but carefully behind the concealing expanse of Martha Wolinski's quivering shoulders – Martha and a mud-coloured baby snake that had poked its head out of her pencil case were regarding each other in mutual horror. Rita had to be mindful of telltale crackles, as there was no predicting what Roger Christopher would do if he caught you passing notes in class. He might make you eat it, conjugate it, regurgitate it, improvising mercilessly your public humiliation. The note read: *Final test. Meet after school in Boose's field.* Another initiation? *Another?* Okay, she'd do it, whatever it was she'd do it. Didn't they realize that initiation meant entrance and that she *would* find a way into their bunkered and enclosed secret society? She was the inspired and eager wolf at the door, the driving rain that sank like claws into the roof, the insinuating wind that bled itself through the pores in the wall. Keep her out? Not likely. She nodded quickly at Greg. Done.

The other note opened like a dirty hand, scribbles leaking into the creases. A poem. Of sorts.

> Roasts are red
> Violence is blue
> Give me a kiss
> And I'll do it to you.

Rita rolled her eyes. She didn't have to look at Stu Stink to know that his ears were flaming red as poppies. Stu had a 'crush' on Rita, but since his vocabulary was severely limited, and his understanding of words strictly monogamous – none of this fooling around with other meanings for him – she was afraid he might literally squeeze the life out of her with his unbearable lumbering attentions. Maybe it was really her lunches he loved, the route from the stomach to the heart being more direct in the Stink anatomy. Besides, Stu had an evil muse, a ghost writer who did his paperwork for him; he probably couldn't even read the messages he sent her.

Rita signed Dinky's name to the note, crushed it back into a greasy ball, and stuffed it into Martha Wolinski's armpit. Martha shrieked and hopped out of her seat, but was instantly upstaged by Rob Moonie who chose that moment to pitch forward on his desk, face first in his protractor set, stone drunk. At recess he'd spent a whole month's allowance, plus his pop bottle money, buying swigs from Dinky's silver flask. They all craned their necks to see if he'd driven the compass through his head, or maybe skewered his eyeball like a cocktail olive. Roger Christopher reached into the front of his dress and pulled out a dollar bill which he waved like a green flag at Rita, asking her to run down to the Ocean House to buy Rob a cup of coffee. Then he lifted his skirts and stepped back into the wending flow of words, the swift mesmerizing verbal stream that coursed throughout the room. *He sipped with his straight mouth*, Rita heard as she flew out the door. *Softly drank through his straight gums, into his slack long body.* There were wings on her heels, a ticket to freedom in her hand. *Silently.* And in the corner of her eye, Dinky Stink watching her, on his face a smile deep as a cut.

Spotted Dick

HIS EYES WERE two jellyfish skulking in the channels and inlets of the Ocean House menu. Two fish eggs looking for a place to hatch. Two orbs of light scanning an unpromising surface. Two run-of-the-mill eyeballs lodged in sockets of unremarkable circumference, searching for something to eat. Innis C. George took predation seriously. He liked to stalk his dinner, hunt it down and run it into the ground, if only vicariously, sleuthing through the underbrush of a restaurant menu. Personally, he preferred a cuisine with spunk, food that fought back, that had some bite of its own (though not like that bowl of chicken soup he'd gotten in the hospital with a pair of dentures grinning up at him from the bottom, noodles undulating between the clamped teeth like worms). He liked spicy, spiny, *dangerous* food, equivocating even as it nourished you, tempting you with a smouldering or explosive illness if you swallowed some alien forbidden part of its anatomy, its rat-black seeds or hairy pit. That a meal might take you for an hallucinogenic ride, or even do you in, was a definite bonus, a culinary thrill particularly gratifying for someone raised on three solid squares a day. As a boy, supper and stupefaction had been synonymous to Innis. He would gaze dully at the heaped mounds that appeared on his Melmac plate, the nightly non-performance of the bland and predictable on a pale green stage, and it was difficult then for him to believe that there was more to life and its weary maintenance than meatloaf and boiled peas. Travel had opened his eyes and his mouth. Starved for a more sophisticated diet, he avidly educated his palate in devouring course after course of Curried Cream of Emerald Soup, *Fiori di Zucca Ripieni Fritti Borgo San Felice*, and Leek-Enrobed Pompano drizzled with Roasted Beet Sauce until his tongue was gastronomically fluent. With it he probed the gustatory edge, nibbled on the exotic and the extreme. He had eaten chiles with volcanic temperaments that turned his stomach acids into seething, erupting lava. He had sampled starfruit that tasted like disinfectant and could be used to clean copper pots. He ventured gamely into the territory of the deadly fugu, capable of causing total paralysis and premature burial – with each thrilling bite he imagined clods of earth raining down on his coffin, the wily blowfish still at large in his system, digesting with excruciating delay, its smirk the last thing to wink out. Yes, Innis had eaten pure unadulterated pain, he had breathed fire, felt his face go numb, watched his hands turn blue. Dining could be a hair-raising experience and he was certainly game, but never before had his eyes ranged over a menu that listed one of its entrées, simply and unashamedly, as *Rubber*.

Food for thought? What about this tersely butchered item – *Meat*? There was a point-blank prose style at work here, obviously penned by some Hemingway of the bill-of-fare genre. Most of the food sounded like hardware. Or crime. What on earth was *Chokedog*? Or *Break and Enter*? Lobster? Probably not. Clearly he needed help, an interpreter to crack the code, but the waitress was busy at the counter with that kid, a frowning intense girl of about ten who had come bursting through the door spilling over with an excited splash of words like someone running with a full pail of water. *In a dress*, he heard, and *drunk*, before the tale trickled into a discreet evaporating whisper. An alcoholic mother, squandered welfare money, neglect – *look* at the child's hair – Innis didn't have to hear the story, standard in a place like this, to know it. He returned his attention to the crude mysteries of the menu, rocked back and forth on his wobbly chair, flicked the silver tongue of the sugar dispenser, stared at the grains of tapioca nesting like ant eggs in the salt shaker, explored with his knee the cordillera of gum buildup under the Arborite tabletop. Peter Inch flashed through his mind like a streaker, and was gone. Finally the kid left, having been loaded down with candy bars, a comic, an ice-pack, several coffees-to-go (*caffeine!* a firing squad of synapses ejaculated prematurely in his head). The waitress was obviously a maternal type on overdrive. Okay, it was *his* turn for some good old-fashioned fussing and mothering.

When she charged over to his table, her huge loopy grin tacked slightly higher onto the one cheek with the dimple, he was ready to dun her with a look of exasperated impatience, a reproving and long-suffering look that would unhinge the grin and make the mouth cohere around those soft round syllables of apology he so richly deserved. He would have, too, if she hadn't been travelling at such a clip, a steaming globe-shaped coffee pot clenched in her fist like a bowling ball aimed straight at his head. He gripped the table and winced, expecting to have his face burned off, his features melting into his hands drip by dissolving drip. He'd *seen* this waitress in action, tripping over chair legs and whacking her hips on the counter. She appeared to have a headlong klutzy intimacy with the material world, a breezy exaggerated disregard for physical boundaries. He bet she was the kind of woman who rammed her feet through her pantyhose getting dressed in the morning. He'd watched her plunk down one customer's meal so hard that half the guy's dinner had jumped off the plate into an ashtray. Given its bounce, Innis wondered if this was the rubber entrée.

'More coffee?' A swill of the scalding brew flew out of the pot and dove with a soft *thup* into the paper napkins.

'I (whew!) haven't actually had any yet.'

'Don't blame you for that. Can't stand the stuff myself. You know what the smell reminds me of? Skunk. Skunk sprayed in a cup. You ready to order?'

'Not yet.'

'Need more time?'

'Hardly. I have a few questions. What's this on the menu here? All it says is *Frank*.'

'Frank? He's in the deep-freeze. You would have liked him, he was a real pet. I'm not sure what's left, though, we had a run on him last week. Want me to check?'

'*No*, that's okay, I'll pass on Frank. How about this?'

'The Stink Special? Prune juice for starters, rump roast with dirty rice no veg, apple slump or blueberry grunt for dessert. And a toothpick.'

'Interesting. What's the *Johnson & Johnson?*'

'Turkey. But it tastes like Band-Aids.'

'*H.M. Meatballs?*'

'You bet.'

'I mean what's the H. M. stand for? Not Her Majesty's, I presume?'

'Nope. Heimlich manoeuvre. They're big.'

'Right. And this?'

'Leftovers.'

'Hmmm.'

Every time she bent over the menu to look, the brimming pot in her hand tipped slightly and sent a thin stream of coffee whishing past his head and splatting onto the floor, freckling his shoes and pantlegs. If only to divert her from shifting close enough to pour it into his ear, he said, 'Maybe I'll hazard a cup of that.'

'It's your funeral.' She flipped the cup upright on the saucer and dumped some coffee in its general vicinity.

'Ow!'

'Oops. Sorry 'bout that. Your hand okay? Don't want to send you back to the hospital.'

'How did you know I was in the hospital?' Innis sucked the heel of his hand as he tried to edge out of the menacing range of her attentions.

'My sister saw you.'

'She a nurse?'

'No. A Stink.'

'Stink?'

'By marriage. Same as the old gal in the bed next to yours. You know the one, done to a turn?'

'Ah, Granny. LaBelle. Stink, eh? I keep hearing that name, it's everywhere.'

'Like a bad smell.'

'You're not one, I take it?'

'Like a disease. Huh? *You kidding?*' She slapped down the coffee pot and it hit the table with a gritty crack, making Innis jump. 'I'm a Stronghill. *Liz* Stronghill.' And this seemed to Liz such a glorious thing to say, crowning the moment with the gold of her name, that she grabbed a chair and wrote herself energetically into it, in body language a billboard-sized signature.

'I see,' said Innis primly, himself a contained and illegible script. He stared at Liz, submerging her in a pool of dream water, holding her under until her persistent and irritating smile rounded into a scream. Not that he had murderous intent – would *he* do that? – but there flickered in her face a teasing resemblance to someone, a disturbing familiarity that he needed to focus and clarify. 'Your sister, what's her name?'

'Ruthie.'

Ruthie. How he hated diminutives and nicknames. Why add a ridiculous trivializing syllable onto a name, like tacking on an ass's tail. But *Ruth*. That name had substance, the weight of a stone in his mouth.

'You here on vacation, or what?'

'Research.'

'Gynaecological?' Liz bit her lip. Somehow that didn't sound right.

'Genealogical, you mean?'

'Yeah. That's it.'

'You could say so.' Innis smiled faintly. He suspected it would take a battering ram of a hint to dislodge her, so comfortably settled with her feet stuck out and crossed at the ankles, one arm flung over the back of the chair, the other in motion, fingers sweeping through her hair. 'Um, shouldn't you be getting back to your customers?'

'Nah. They can take care of themselves. I got 'em trained.'

Behaviour modification, no doubt. He glanced around to see if anyone else had been scalded or maimed. A guy with an angry swelling clapped onto the side of his head was scrabbling around in the cutlery, setting a table, while another stood at the cash, punching in his bill, holding it awkwardly in the hand with the splint. A quick survey revealed scars, a black eye, broken limbs, and a number of diners who appeared to be unconscious. Though the place did seem to be possessed of a remarkable self-sufficiency.

'How are the tips?'

'Not bad. Considering.'

'*Say*,' Innis leaned forward, having taken a sudden keen interest in Liz's chest. '*Where* did you get those? They're *very* nice.'

'*Excuse me?*' He did say *tips*, didn't he?

'I bet they're real. You don't mind if I have a closer look, do you? I'd love to examine them.'

Liz gaped at him, and at the bracken-brown top of his head – what did he part his hair with, a fork? It's not that she wasn't used to this sort of hassle – and *not* that she couldn't deal with it – but she had expected from him something in the way of style, the usual crudities, locally and abundantly available, smoothed and polished into a rare and slick approach.

'Lovely.' He leaned back. 'How old are they?'

'Old?'

'They look ancient. Let's just say they've been around for a while, eh? How much would you like for them?'

Raising her hand protectively to shield her body from further insult and proposition, Liz grazed the two brass buttons that decorated the front pocket flaps of her dress. 'Oh, *these*.'

'Where did you say you got them?' *What* marvellously embossed gorgon faces.

'From Holmes.'

'Holmes?' Writhing snaky locks.

'Stink.'

'Another Stink?' Tiny terrible mouths, plugged with centuries of dirt.

'Afraid so.'

'Where would a Stink find something like this?' He wondered if he should offer to buy her dress.

'In the lake. Same place he finds everything. Same place he found you.'

'Me?' Clearly, she didn't know their value.

'Good as dead till he dragged you up.'

'I had no idea.' He'd *have* them. 'And you say he does salvage work?'

'Yeah. Heard *you* lost something?'

'That's right. I wouldn't mind getting it back, either.'

'Really? Don't you think it's a little late for that? I mean, a fish might have eaten it, or something?'

'I doubt that. It was pretty hard.'

'*Oh!*' Ruthie had warned her about this guy. She had an allergy to perverts, too. Couldn't get within spitting distance of Tennessee Ernie without breaking out in hives.

'Where are you going?'

The snappy pinhole-eyed Gorgon faces glared at him as they shot past. 'Back to work, what do you think? That I can sit around here all day like Lady Jane? La-di-dah? See, Albert's into the pie again. That man loves his cherry. *Someone* has to slap his wrists.'

'What about my dinner?'

'What about it?'

'I *want* it.'

Liz tossed her head in annoyance, her scalp beginning to prickle and itch. She marched over to the next table and whipped a plate out from under a man's rapidly descending spoon, which then tapdanced across the Arborite like a blind man's cane.

'Awww, Liz.'

'Stop snivelling. You've had enough.' She strode back to Innis's table and slapped the plate down with such force that it spun before his eyes. 'Is this what you're looking for?'

'You can't be serious? It's half eaten. There's *hair* in it. What *is* it?'

'Spotted dick.'

'But it's … it's … *disgusting*.'

'Exactly.'

The Blue Room

THE BLUE ROOM had many fine appointments. A Louis XIII mahogany armchair, a recumbent crystal chandelier, an intact Harry Clarke stained-glass window, a Hepplewhite claw-footed armoire that contained a silver watch case, a scarf pin, a French brass escutcheon in the shape of a sea horse, a Queen Victoria cake plate, and a pair of breeches. Sitting on top of the armoire was a nineteenth-century Dewey-Gridley commemorative pitcher that had a high pouring lip (chipped), an ear-shaped handle, a decorative motif of mortar shells encircling the base, and the following inscription: *You may fire when ready, Gridley.* The pitcher was filled to the top of Admiral George Dewey's embossed and transparent head with a burden of glass eyes which stared out madly at skewed angles scattering vision like buckshot. Within the liquid walls of the Blue Room – paintings had to be launched rather than hung – you could also find a birch cradle (birch to ward off evil spirits, though not eels), a crate of tubas, a cannon rammer, a severed wooden hand holding a wooden ball, a reclining rocker, and a gutted television set with bunny ears and a resident test pattern of rock bass.

Resting several fathoms below the town dock, the Blue Room was an anthology of secrets, a miscellany of objects each with its own unidentified story coiled in stubborn silence around it. Water had absolved this odd collection of ownership, though not of history. Tumbling out of boats – wracked, scuttled, swamped, torn in two – falling out of hands fond or grasping, as rings might slip off water-washed fingers, these things had unwed themselves from human need and desire. Even before Holmes found them and carried them to his blue room, his rec room below the *Marylou*, they had become part of a new underwater decor, call it early Lakebed. And though the patina of use, of finger-prints and sweat, the smear of the corruptible, had long been stripped from their surfaces, they still retained a ghostly veneer of potential narrative that was almost legible to Holmes. He wasn't a treasure hunter, having open hands himself, giving easy passage, so much as a curator and temporary guardian. An anthologist of unreadable stories.

That would be him appearing out of a billowing silt-roused cloud with a figurehead in his arms, a blind Cassandra of the lake trailing dark undulate willow moss like a widow's tattered dress, like the fronds of her own tragedy, her eggshell-blue eyes eaten away. Once, her ears might have been filled like little demitasse cups with the lamentations and confessions of doomed men, men crawling along a heaving deck in terror to supplicate a wooden woman. Her ears, lovely vessels conducting their prayers – fear-filled and thick as a sickly-sweet liqueur – to heaven. (More likely their messages would have taken a more circuitous route, spilling out of her ears and into the lake, their strength diluted as they passed like jokes through the gills and urinary tracts of fish, in time evaporating, travelling skyward more as contented sighs than desperate pleas for help.) She was an orphan now, and if alive and sensate would marvel at this swimmer who bore her in his arms over an invisible threshold into a well and eccentrically furnished bower. If sighted, she might stare in wonder at him, as many a passerby did strolling along the dock on a clear fine day, gazing into the water, hoping to catch a glimpse of a perch or some minnows, and seeing instead a *room* down there – *Surely that's not a lamp? Not a Persian carpet?!* – and in that room a masked fin-footed idler stretched out on a reclining rocker reading a fluttery-leaved book or watching TV, puffing away on his air supply like a man with a hookah.

Say what you will about the Blue Room, it had character. Character, but no atmosphere. Didn't matter to Holmes. He adapted easily to wearing his lungs on his back, like an anatomically peculiar fish. For the lake, sure he would give up even his breath, it was his dream home and his dream country. Air was exile. Water caressed him in perpetual welcome. One time, before his cousin Gram and Ruthie Stronghill were married, he escaped the tentacled, strangling hold of a double date by disappearing into the very heart of it. Gram had steered Ruthie and her friend, the cumbersome Cindy, down to the dock, where he must have figured that the lapping and seductive patter of the lake would undo them, or at least their clothes. But it was Holmes who was seduced, who slipped like a bound and gagged Houdini out of Cindy's suffocating embrace, stepped swiftly to the edge of the dock, and then *in*, straight down, submerging himself – all ears – in the water's black silken speech. *Hey, shithead, where d'you think you're going?* Gram stood spluttering and cursing on the dock, watching his dumb cousin's noggin bob like a liberated buoy in the channel, fleeing on the crest of the night.

Holmes laughed to think of it still, though you had to be careful laughing underwater – you could drown, a happy fool. He kept his amusement contained, like life-giving oxygen concealed in tanks, all those monosyllabic exclamations jammed in his head, the preserves of utter joy. Sometimes to diffuse the pressure he wrote them down on a slate – *Ha ha ha!* – feeling like Jack Horner pulling plums out of a pie. Oh yes, his Blue Room suited him well. One thing, he didn't have to dust. The room washed itself like a cat, and on occasion even redecorated, shifting things about or sweeping them back out to the depths of the lake, never to be seen again. Boredom was something Holmes simply didn't feel below the waterline. In fact, he had come to the conclusion that boredom was a land word, a high and dry word that in the water softened and changed, becoming an interesting unparched blossoming bearer of fruit. When Holmes dove backwards off the deck of the *Marylou*, he entered an element of pure fascination. He could spend hours floating around looking at things, standing on his head, or playing games with the bass, those Nosy Parkers of the finny population. Weightlessness helped. Underwater, the leaden anchoring ego lightened, its nagging heft eased up and you were freer, available to become part of whatever was going on around you. Even a mirror propped against the pilings below reflected the self differently, otherly, as a shadow enfolded in a dim loveliness.

The Blue Room was a fine place to think things over and Holmes often came down with a single word in mind and let it bat around in his head as he considered it. He liked especially to bring down pieces of the sky. As in *starling*. He could say it over and over *starling starling starling* until it metamorphosed into a near endearment. And how wonderfully odd, he thought, that such a pretty nursery rhymish sort of word should become the verbal roost of those slangy avian greaseballs, those Elvis impersonators of the air, those black flapping rags torn out of the night. Because really, starlings were stupid and common as dirt. A beautiful name clothing a seedy and suspect character. Like *starfish*, their cute etymological cousins, that were actually voracious devourers of the unlucky drowned, vultures of the deep that grew plump as pillows on human provender. *Provender*. How full and nourishing that word sounded, and how like *provenance*, one of his favourites. *Prov-e-nan-ce*, Holmes would think, stretching and prodding the soft body of the word's meaning like a snail tugged out of a shell. Origins, beginnings, a fertile loamy linguistic bed out of which anything could arise, a garden of possibilities. Though as for his own provenance, he probably knew more, or at least divined more, about the found objects in his Blue Room than he did about himself. Take the rocking chair, for instance. Built in a factory in Owen Sound by a man who constructed well-upholstered odes to lumber during his lunch break, shipped to a warehouse in Toronto where nightly the watchman dozed on it and dreamt of his former girlfriend Lucy of the capacious thighs, transported to Butt's Furniture on the Island, and finally bought by Ellen Lewis for her husband Ted for Father's Day (*from the kids xox*). A siren in Naugahyde as it turned out. Poor old Ted couldn't walk past the chair without being lured into its padded mobile bulk, riding it incline to upright repeatedly until the thing drove Ellen nuts. Late one night, she and the kids wrestled it onto the back of Ted's truck, drove down to the dock and dumped it in the lake. It sank slowly, listing to the bottom in a regal descent, and settled in the Blue Room, a throne tempting and comfy enough to suit Poseidon himself. Now that was provenance *and* Providence rolled into one.

A true story. True enough. More fact than Holmes felt he could muster for himself, at any rate, there being more fiction in his blood than corpuscles. Over the years he had heard so much about his mother from his Stink relations that she seemed to be made mostly of story. She was a figure compounded of images. Emmy the gypsy, climbing out of her bedroom window at night to sleep in the fields. Emmy the extortionist, the pirate queen of the schoolyard, her pockets bulging with juvenile booty. Emmy the whirlwind, rushing off to a dance wearing a half-finished dress, carrying the buttons in her hand, the zipper flung over her shoulder. She wore her clothes like cutouts, anyway. They kept falling off. And *voilà* ... Holmes! If Emmy was a story, a dissatisfying inconclusive one at that, then his father was a one-word poem – the less said the better. *Hell, I never even knew she was knocked up*, said her mother, LaBelle Stink. *Didn't slow down long enough for me to get a good look at her.* Memory and dream feed into one another, creating a stir that lifts her up to the roof of the barn as if on a light wind. Was it true? Did she really, six months gone, walk a tightrope, a clothesline strung from the barn to the cowshed, holding a rake handle for balance, an owl's wild hoot forming in her mouth? Or that other time, after he was born, did she really toss him high into the air and let him fall, let him plummet like a foundering cupid, his baby blanket unfurling him into nakedness as he pitched headfirst into the duck pond? Was she the one responsible for his first wondrous and besotted view of underwater life, his first caddis worms, ramshorn snails, diving beetles, frog spawn like a clump of eyes that stared back at his two enormous blue ones? Or was it all simply some tale his cousins Gram and Chet embroidered in the layered heat of the attic bedroom he shared with them? The dark conducted lies with a galvanizing ease. They pretended that the words hurt them, too, handling them like knife blades, pointing inward. But Holmes knew the pleasure they took in telling him how very much she hated him and how she had tried to drown him, only Uncle Burton scooped him out of the pond with a fish net, and said *Emmy, you fucken slut*, and she just smiled and walked away. Holmes preferred to take the smile and leave the rest, curling himself up in it like a hammock slung in midair. It was only a story, anyway. Dissolvable in water. The immersed journal of his childhood, ink drifting like smoke off the pages, letters undoing like slipknots releasing their captive sentiments, subsuming them in something wider and bluer and more dangerously real.

Now *her* stories, he remembered those, even though the teller had long since withdrawn up the slab-hard steps of her own words. The memory of her physical presence might have come apart for him, but he could still hear her voice clearly, a strong definable current snaking through the air. This of course had a lot to do with the kind of stories she told. Not hard-luck stories so much as bad luck, tough and stark, unrelieved by whimsy. As a young boy he would struggle against sleep, fight it for all he was worth, but she would heap on him a dead weight of fact that would take him straight to the bottom every time. She felled him nightly, sent him to the kingdom of oblivion with stories of car crashes, sea disasters, random violence. Identifying with the luckless heroes of these reports, he'd be ripped apart and decapitated. He went down with the *Asia* and the *Baltimore*, washing ashore with acres of cans, bales of hay, bloated grain, and corpses, knocking against them hard as merchandise. Times he was frozen to the others in a cluster, their heads capped in ice, battered ragged on the rocks. What he got from her was not exactly *Cinderella* or *The Three Little Pigs*. And what he got was not exactly forgettable.

Holmes carries with him this memory of Emmy leaving, solid and real as the holy medal worn round his neck. She is blasting out of the bay in the Stink outboard, throttle wide open, cutting the glassy calm of the water in two, breaking it like a huge mirror. He stands on the shore watching her go, her black hair lashing behind her. At six years of age he is still young enough to think he can extend his will as far as his vision. Like a believer supplicating a statue, he prays to her. *Stop. Please turn around. Oh please.* But if a statue bends to your will, softens and smiles, grants you your wish, well, that's a miracle. She doesn't stop. She doesn't even turn around to look at him one last time so that he might remember her face, a cameo now horribly riddled and corroded. Water damaged.

He didn't watch her go, naturally. No one did. She simply stepped into the night and ducked under its black wing. Gone. In the morning, the outboard was still there, gently nudging the shore, its painter tied securely around a rock. At bedtime the evening before she took off, she told Holmes the story of the *Courtlandt* and the *Morning Star*, a schooner and a paddlewheel steamer that collided in the dead of night 1868, one of the *Courtlandt*'s crew members having taken down her running lights to clean them. She was invisible. The *Morning Star* rammed her broadside. She swung round and crashed into the steamer's churning paddles, which tore a great gaping hole in her side. Both ships sank. *No survivors*, Emmy said flatly. Then she said, 'You can have my worms.'

'Huh?'

'Don't say *huh*.'

'What?'

'My worms. Take them.' She held out an old ice cream bucket. 'Don't you want them?'

'I'm sick of fishing. You catch a fish for me, eh? A nice big one, a muskie.'

'You mean it? Wow, *thanks*.'

'I gotta go now, okay?'

Holmes hugged the bucket tight as a teddy bear to him, thrilled. Emmy knew where to find the *best* bait. He kept lifting the lid to peek inside where the fat pink crawlers were tucked in their own soft mossy bed, and he drifted off to sleep like that, clutching the worm bucket, the grin on his face itself sharp as a hook. He might have even caught a dream-fish with that grin, if it hadn't bent out of shape as the nights passed, losing its edge as he clutched the bucket tighter and tighter until he crushed it entirely, the worm rot creeping out. And *boy* did it smell, a real stomach-flipping stench, same as when Gram killed that puppy and hid him under the bed so no one would find out.

It's not that Emmy didn't have maternal attributes. In a way she was always preparing Holmes for the worst – and then she did it. She was like a boulder rolled out of the sky that had smashed to bits his sense of who he was and where he belonged. (Not usually a Stink affliction. A Stink was a Stink, as a dog was a dog, a snake a snake, etc.) Even his notion of what constituted a home was scattered, arrayed across the town and out across the lake like an exploded view. His address was wide, encompassing Stinkville, the Ocean House bar, the swing bridge, the *Marylou*, a lilac bush beside the Catholic church he liked to sleep under, the Shaftsbury Hall (Holmes was a dancer, that's who he was), the Blue Room, and the extension where Emmy lived, that sprawling multi-roomed mansion that was the rest of the world. Holmes could hang his hat anywhere, on a deer antler, untrophied and charging through the bush, on a branch drifting downstream, it was all the same to him. He knew that a house, a thing so tightly conceived, room flush against room, could drive a person crazy. Women threw themselves out of windows, down wells, to escape the claustrophobic masculine hug of a house. He had watched Gram's wife Ruthie pacing from one room to the next, up stairs and down, restless as water slapping against the walls. And Rita, she could yank her uncle right out of the grave and through the woodwork of that rickety place the Cabals rented over on Draper, just to furnish her conviction that she didn't belong there. She could animate the watermarks on the ceiling, make them stretch and spin, and make the carpets bleed, and the furniture shift and sidle, so charged and credulous was her sight. (Maybe it was true she saw more, fear rounding her eyes, letting in whatever skirted the edges.) When Holmes first saw Rita he thought she was a water-lily, her communion dress blossoming around her as she floated down, drowning with such self-possession, not letting her life jerk awkwardly out of her mouth in panic, that he didn't realize what she was doing. Visitors did drop in occasionally, mostly kids swimming off the town dock. Rita was more surprised to see him. Holmes was in the Blue Room playing a game of one-man chess, but having trouble with the crayfish, unreliable and erratic bishops, scooting away and shying under the marble board. She had hardly expected *this*, and was amazed, though didn't want to show it. She *had* seen stranger things, after all.

'I can't swim,' she told Holmes later on board the *Marylou*, wrapped in a scratchy Hudson's Bay blanket and sipping an orange crush into which Holmes had slipped a finger of rum. 'It was a test for Chamuel. He's supposed to be watching over me. He should have saved me. But do you know where he is? Out behind the drug store picking through garbage cans. He's got filthy habits.'

Holmes took this in, nodding. He invested little belief in angels himself. 'What was he looking for?'

Rita narrowed her eyes to determine if Holmes was making fun of her. 'Who knows. Dirty magazines? He's inscrutable.'

'He would be, wouldn't he?' Inscrutable, eh? His tongue travelled the contours of the word, checking its weight, handling it like a greengrocer examining a peach for imperfections. A word like this, something you can really sink your teeth into, it might come in handy.

Rita grinned, suddenly struck with happiness, the source of it seeming to come from behind her knees, a weird sensation of helium pumping up her calves, the finger of rum lifting that oppressive heaviness in her that had taken her to the bottom of the lake. She *liked* Holmes. Any other adult would question her possession of such language, as if she'd swiped it and had no right to use it. They would make her pay with some mocking comment, sharp shaming words meant to cut her down to size. But Holmes was glad of it, buoyant in a pool of afternoon sun, squelching water in his ear with his baby finger, savouring the word sweet as a secret in his mouth, grinning back at her.

'More rum?' he asked.

After that, Rita had an open invitation to the Blue Room through which she swam freely. Swimming came to her swiftly as an idea igniting her arms and legs – she could do it! Looking up from his rocking chair, Holmes would see her jackknife like a streak of lightning through his ceiling. Or she would shatter it with a cannonball, her small tender body hugging itself into a round bone-hard missile.

He taught her the fundamentals of diving, how to use the equipment and the decompression tables, and they practised buddy breathing. But she preferred to swim unencumbered, testing the limits of what was humanly possible. She imagined herself a pearl diver, stretching the seconds out longer and longer until they snapped like elastics and propelled her gasping to the surface. Holmes made sure she understood what would happen to her if she blacked out underwater, but he didn't nag her about it. He gave her the information she needed to survive and let her do what she liked with it. He had no intention of becoming a parent, a creature as unreal and spooky to him as any spectre Rita herself could dream up. When he was down he preferred to stay down, but Rita worried the water constantly. She was in and out, diving over and over, toes curled on the edge of the dock, hands raised in a delicate steeple, applying herself to the fabric of the lake as though stitching her very being into it.

A child will knock the stuffing – and stuffiness – out of any home, stirring things up, making the air throb with life. And so it seemed to Holmes that a new and unknown current now mingled with the familiar ones that muscled into the Blue Room and spirited away his dearest discoveries right from under his masked nose. *Heck*, the Blue Room had no doors outside of a few stacked here and there, certainly none you could close and lock. He missed her when she didn't stop by, though 'stop' was a word you could hardly apply to Rita. He kept an eye out, watching for her, which is why he spotted Innis George snooping around before Innis saw *him*. Innis on the dock, squinting into the water, a dress draped over his arm. A *familiar* dress, pie-sized polka dots, brass buttons, the wind picking lightly at it. Treading water, concealed behind the backside of the *Marylou*, Holmes studied his visitor. He'd heard the guy had a problem, but really, a *dress*? Maybe he'd just murdered someone, by accident of course, same as how he flipped his car into the channel. He had a strong family resemblance to *trouble*. A shitload of it, some of which Holmes had already sampled on the guy's puffy lips when he'd resuscitated him, exchanging the life in his own lungs for dead man's breath. It had been like inhaling a fetid stinking rag into his chest.

Holmes pushed himself back silently into the water. Living in a broken home wasn't so bad when you considered the cracks through which you can escape, the eternally long hallways, the unexplored and far-flung rooms. He felt an urgent need to visit the romantic and dispersed ruins of such a home. A placeless place in which he might make himself scarce. Invisible, even. Like the *Courtlandt*, only more deft and attuned to potential disaster. I know what I am, he thought. I'm ... *inscrutable*, and he sank out of sight, following this definition of himself like a sounding line, down, down deeper and away into the dark and pliable corners of the lake.

Innis missed the trail of telltale bubbles Holmes left in his wake, but noticed a rope tied to the dock that appeared to have an object dangling on its end. When he hoisted it out of the water, reeling in what he must have thought was a genuine catch, possibly some priceless treasure Holmes had unwittingly discovered, he found himself holding a slate on which someone had written the singularly puerile message, *Ha ha ha!*

Ladyfingers

FIRECRACKERS MAKE THE devils jump. So say the ancient Chinese. So says Roger Christopher, *in* Chinese, so no one gets it. Except Rita, she *gets* it. And they did jump all right. Sky high. Broke rank and blew apart, hightailed it, skedaddled, flew away to hide under floor boards and up chimneys. They poured themselves like scummy drainwater down cracks, leaked into crevices lowly and thin. Cowards all, trembling if you pointed an accusing finger at them. *She should have let go,* they whine. *No one's that stupid. If she got hurt it's her own fault.* Tiny red horns trembling.

Now you wouldn't go so far as to call a Stink a gentleman, but in the battle of the sexes, even Stinks concede to certain standards of conduct. There are certain things you do to a lady, and certain things you *don't* do. You don't put your greasy paws on the light side of her reversible skirt. (Man, she *hates* that, it makes her spit.) You don't wipe your nose on her bare shoulder, or stick your leftover gum in her hair. Same applies to unsnapping her barrettes, flicking burrs at her ankle socks, or setting her little plastic purse on fire. If you absolutely have to, it's permissible to wear her underpants on your head, legholes looped over your ears, while performing one of those muscular bounding Russian dances you've seen on TV. (Go ahead, make a fool of yourself, she'll *like* that.) But it is definitely not okay to give a lady the back of your hand, to twist her arm until it snaps, to kick her when she's down, or to say, *Here, hold this Cherry Bomb,* while you run off to take sanctuary behind a big rock. It's just not done. Ladies need their fingers. They can do so many things with them, including *nice* things for you. Ah, the Cherry Bomb, the M-80, the Silver Salute, the Thunder Buzzard – fireworks that have launched a thousand fingers. Stinks have been known to scatter a few firecrackers here and there, detonating melons in the garden, blowing the heads off tulips. Indeed, they were pyrotechnic dabblers, but at least they tried to draw the line at drawing blood. (Accidents happened of course, say if they lashed a rocket to a kitten's tail, or stuck a roman candle up a sow's arse.) But those boys, those friends of Rita's, weren't very clever at drawing lines, or making inviolable and airtight that club of theirs, which consisted mainly of words anyway, stuck together with a few licks of information. (*The Snakes?* Roger Christopher queried. *Isn't that a bit obviously phallic? Huh?* they said. *Look it up.*) And Rita was persistent as a roach, determined as any infiltrating vermin to find the breach through which she might enter. She wanted *in*, and would spend her arms and legs to do it. Would stick a ladyfinger like a fag in her mouth and light up. *Would* turn herself inside out, by some corporeal alchemy translate her leaden female self into the dazzling person of a golden-skinned boy. If that was the price. She would do it, just as she had walked in the grave-yard at midnight, eaten a live worm, stuck pins in her arm, drunk her own pee, stood barefoot on broken glass, let them whip her with branches and pelt her with stones. She would mortify and flay and embarrass the flesh right off her body and hand it to them, if only they would let her be one of them.

Her friends weren't heartless, Greg and Ronny and Rob, but sol-dered together (with power, not grace) they formed an unholy trin-ity. Fused at joint and muscle, nerves spliced, brains interwired, they were a minor monstrosity, a cubbed-together machine that once set in motion they didn't know how to stop. They wished she would simply go away. The message they gave her couldn't be clearer, *bam*, square in the face every time, and yet she still didn't *get* it. Nothing she could ever do would gain her admittance into their club. She would have to *die* first. She would have to die and be reborn, re-emerging splendid and triumphant, festooned with male parapher-nalia. Would she do *that*?

'Shit, man,' Dinky Stink said, scything his lean self through head high (*his* head) couch-grass, cuckoo spit smeared up his arm, froghoppers mired in a permanent crawl on the slick Brylcreemed crest of his hair. Without his car he felt plucked naked, but had resisted the impulse to peel through Boose's field and rip out his transmission, rocks being one of the Boose's main crops. His nose twitched, an acrid burn smell coiling up into it thick as hair. He'd heard the blast, a cracking report like an engine backfiring, and had seen those little drips pelt through the field helter-skelter. Dinky himself was a lethal explosive packed into a deceptively slight frame, a cellular concoction deadly as any mix of gunpowder and nitroglyc-erin, topped up with a sprinkle of TNT. One of these days he was going to open up and fill the sky with fireworks of his own, the

Dinky Dazzler mushrooming into a stunningly tall and well-hung display. He could feel the pressure building in the top of his head, hormones boiling right under his scalp – *you wait, he was gonna grow!* Dinky even carried a tape measure in his back pocket next to his mammoth gap-toothed yellow comb in the event he should have to do some emergency measuring.

A brushy sprig of timothy poked him in the eye, practically putting out that gleam in it, which caused him to yank the plant up by the roots, bite off its head and grind it between his teeth, spitting the shreds off his tongue like tobacco. Boose's field was a fucken jungle, *why* was he doing this? Why had the need to see Rita Cabal, to simply *see* her, come upon him so suddenly that he laid enough rubber on the highway to make himself a wet suit? Why did the hairs prickle on the back of his neck, and the sweat dance out of his palms like blood out of a cut? She was cute all right, wiry and snappy, but not his type. (His cousin Stu thought she was *his* type, but Dinky figured a girl would have to be knock-kneed, buck-toothed and blind to be Stu's type.) Nope, Dinky liked 'em big and blonde. He liked to stand under them like scaffolding, a breast in each hand, maybe a single one resting on his head like a huge meaty tam. A halo of flesh accessorizing Saint Dinky, patron of the mature figure, *yeah*. And Rita was only a kid. Was that it? She was an eighth of an inch shorter than he was, and an eighth of an inch is nothing to sneeze at. It made him feel positively heroic, a towering figure of a man. Besides, he'd scrapped and fought for every eighth of an inch he'd gained in the world and didn't want to see a bunch of baby-faced pricks steal from Rita what was rightfully hers. Though, fuck. Why play natureboy, Tarzan of the back forty? He should beat it, scram, get the hell out of here, mind his own beeswax. Where he *should* be was in the Ocean House leaning back in a chair and sucking his teeth after a good feed of fries and gravy (gotta eat if you wanna grow), and eyeing Liz Stronghill, who with luck might still be waiting tables wearing her slip .

But no. No, too late. In the clearing.

'Shit, man,' he said again. '*Shit.*'

Running now, tearing at his shirt, buttons zinging off. A hank of ripped cloth flowing white as a corporal in his hand. It behoves a Stink to know a thing or two about first aid, what with their demolition-derby approach to the road, their Saturday night punch-ups, and the company their hides generally keep with sharp and unstable objects.

They weren't interns but close enough, having done their time in emergency wards keeping their ears cocked and their eyes peeled – providing they were still conscious and those eyes weren't too swollen to open. So as Dinky approached the crumpled bundle, Rita as ragdoll flung in the grass, he knew he had to get that arm up. You gotta keep your wounds higher than your heart, right, an old Stink maxim. And he knew not to tie a tourniquet, but to use the swath torn off his shirt to stopper the hand before she poured her life out of her arm like a tipped teapot. He could almost hear it whisper away into the grass. 'Hey, *kid*.' Apply pressure. Check pulse. Count her fingers. Her *fingers*, holy shit! How many gone? Two. Thumb and index. Aw *Christ*, a girl's gotta have those. How's she supposed to dial the phone, test the soup? Think of Amanda Hook, Captain Hook as she was known, who harrowed your back with her wicked pitchfork nails, raking up your freckles and moles into bleeding burning heaps. How diminished the effect with two tines missing. Those two. A missing baby finger is no big deal. Stunted, cocked for status, the poodle of the pack, a mere decoration in Dinky's opinion. You could always clean your ears out with a nut pick if worse came to worst. If it was her pinky that had taken a hike, he wouldn't bother, or that other one, the drone next to the middle finger, next to the *finger* finger. Both useless. But Tommy Thumb and Peter Pointer … better find 'em.

Dinky scuffed around in the grass. He had a good eye, and anyway, he figured all he'd have to do was look for a concentration of flies, a distillation of noisy verminous passion. Fly interest would be keen. The arrival of detached human fingers was surely an event that surpassed other celestial windfalls, more wondrous even than cow flaps or dead birds. *Buzz, buzz* … and yes, right *there*, that was one of them. Rita's index finger curled around the stem of a daisy as though poised for plucking it. And over *there*, wasn't that the other, her torn thumb, so homely and grub-like? So small it looked more easily like something that would devour a leaf, sprout wings, and fly away, than be used to hitch a ride out of town. Amazing really, when you thought about it, the thumb. Dinky couldn't help but identify with the sturdy little digit. Strong and versatile, and damned articulate for an appendage. Thumbs up or down, asserting approval or dissent. Useful for insults, for comfort, for getting things into perspective, for punctuating the grooviest of tunes at Stink singalongs. Mitch Miller. Perry Como. Hard to be cool without a thumb.

But hey. *Shit*. He'd better move it, get Rita into town, and fast. Dinky scooped up the stray digits and secured them in his shirt front pocket. Then carefully as if Rita were already fatally fractured, he scooped her up too, and gently so as not to have her come apart in his arms, he began to run. In the pocket of his ripped and bloodied shirt, her cradled finger and thumb swung free, tap tapping against his chest, knocking out a lively tattoo in sync with his accelerating heartbeat as he tore through the field toward his car.

Blake Hardy had fish lips. Not like a smallmouth or a pike, but his soft nibbly lips grazing her fingertips would remind Liz of minnows in warm shallow water bussing and tickling her legs and toes. Sometimes he got carried away, licking her fingers right up to the webs, chewing on her knuckles, sucking on her palms like they were oyster shells. After a heavy date she'd have to sneak into the house with her hands shoved in her armpits. She was the only one in highschool with hickeys on her mount of Venus, her fingertips wrinkled as raisins. She felt like Lady Macbeth always rubbing her hands together, plastering lotion on them, which Blake must have swallowed a gallon of, not to mention the pound of nail polish he scraped off with his teeth. *Ladyfingers*, he'd growl, *yum yum*, falling on all fours and slinking toward her. She'd scream in anticipation and throw her skirt up over her head. They acted dumb, that's for sure. Like a couple of kids. (Which they were.) *I've come to ask for your hand*, Blake would say solemnly, then pretend to saw it off at the wrist while they both shrieked and snorted like maniacs.

Liz wonders what happened to those lips. When Chet Stink's jigsaw jalopy, held together with hockey tape and Bazooka bubble gum, crested Borden's Hill and hit Blake's car dead on, his dad's brand-new Mustang, it was the Ford that crumpled like paper and Blake who flew apart as though there was nothing to it. Of course, hitting a Stink is like slamming into a brick wall. Chet stepped out of his old bomb scratching his empty and unharmed head wondering what had happened, while you had to pick Blake out of the trees. He was everywhere. Flesh falling like snow.

Blake as blizzard. Liz dreams sometimes of gathering him up like broken pieces of crockery and sticking him back together, of putting those dextrous and desirable fingers of hers to good use. But somehow she can never get it right. He ends up being too small, and incomplete. He becomes a baby in her arms crying and crying because he has no lips. He's hungry, he wants her, he wants to suck on her fingers, at least that would quiet him. But she can't find what he needs. She has searched everywhere, inside her dreams and out. She hasn't seen those lips in years.

Liz Stronghill usually walked with a certain degree of swank, tossing her hips freely from side to side, and today was no exception. Why should she trim the fat off her personal ambulatory style just to oblige the tight squeeze of uncomfortable memory? She wished Blake wouldn't follow her around like this, memories of him boiled down to blackfly size, pestering, biting. She'd swing her rear like a cow's tail if she thought she could bat him away. Maybe she was annoyed about selling her dress. *What* had possessed her? Holmes had made that dress for her himself, pedalling away on his rusty reclaimed Singer, shyly bringing it to her in the restaurant wrapped in crackly butcher's paper, the string tied in reef knots. She assumed it was a fish, some fat bass that had fallen asleep in the soft bed of his hands. How *could* she? But twenty bucks is twenty bucks, now sitting like cream filling in the centre of her purse. That Innis guy, the dickless wonder, claimed he wanted it for a 'friend' back home, said his friend had been searching years for a dress like that. With polka dots? And sleeves like puffballs? And a real crooked hem? Holmes had hand-stitched it underwater so that it would 'flow' properly. And he was one of the smarter Stinks. Ah well. The guy wants to dress up in women's clothes that's his business, she wasn't going to publish it in the town paper.

Liz sashayed up Meredith past the hospital toward home, garnering honks and wolf whistles from every carload of guys that passed. Dinky Stink screeched by, the nub of his head barely visible over the steering wheel, his *ooo-ga* horn blasting away, filling the air like a cartoon balloon packed with crude suggestion. *Good Lord*, Liz thought, can't I walk up my *own* street in my own slip without drawing undue and uncalled-for attention to myself? *Men!* Then in view of Dinky's stature, recast her aspersions closer to the ground. *Squirts. Punks. Pimples! Wham, wham*, went her hips, bodychecking a whole minor league of irritants smack into the ditch.

Don't tell me. Not again. Already? Dr Nopper heard Dinky Stink slam on his brakes and skid halfway across the hospital parking lot, an all too familiar fanfare for yet another Stink emergency. How did they do it? He marvelled at the Stink anatomy, that infinitely regenerative thing. How many times had he swabbed, sutured, and stitched it, set bones, pumped stomachs, remarried limbs? One time he even reunited Tennessee Ernie with the tip of his nose bitten off in a fight. He had extracted marbles, pennies, pussy willows and a banana from a range of Stink orifices, not to mention the bean that Burton tried to dig out of his ear with a nut pick, pushed further in – clear into his brain, Dolly said – and forgot about. Of all the strange cases he'd encountered over the years, Burton was his only instance of a man with a plant growing out of the side of his head. Standing by the office window, he had looked positively decorative. Verdant with sunlight splashing like grease over his hair and filtering through his new green appendage. He could easily have passed for a cleverly conceived plant holder you might find in one of the tourist shops downtown.

Stinks approached health care and the nurturance of their bodies the way children played with dolls, yanking off their arms and legs then jamming them back on, jabbing them with knitting needles or whapping them against walls, and no one seemed any the worse for it. Pain was a bad business, life's business, and they were good at it. Professionals who answered its call with a dignified indifference, entertained it in a variety of venues, and never let it get the better of them. You couldn't unnerve them, either. Casually mention to most patients before an operation that *Boy, I'm all thumbs today.* and you'd practically have to pop their eyes back in their sockets for them. But a Stink would only grin and wink, and try to goose the nurse if she wasn't quick enough to knock him out with a sedative first.

Dr Nopper jumped up and rubbed his hands together, hands that had intimate knowledge of Stink clay, that could read their rough bodies like braille, and yet remain open, empty as basins, prepared for *anything*. He never knew what unscripted medical challenge a Stink was going to bring him. Nor could he predict when he was finally, inevitably, going to fumble, spooked by the wild pitch or the unexpected angle, and let one of their many lives slip through his fingers. Better go down and see.

The cloud that floated over Rita darkened and rained down bits and pieces, shreds of herself. Herself, and others, though in no particular order. Feet didn't come first, but a head, horned upside down, red red hissing lips. *Don't tell. Don't tell and we'll let you join our club for sure.* The horns were lit fuses. *Look out!* Rita watched her arms skim past, her ankles fleet as Mercury's, tumbling like dice. She had come apart and was falling to earth in instalments, fragments of shell and bone, buttons blue as bruises, this and that. But someone else was going to have to put her together because her hands hadn't arrived yet. Her mother's face drifted by, distorted with grief, a cut-out tragic mask, her uncle the laughing evil twin. If her skin arrived in sheets, in rolled bolts, she'd ask Holmes to make her a new body. Her toes hit the ground like superballs, *quick*. Her hair in a meteor shower. When the storm was over she would have to count herself to make sure that nothing was missing. *You owe me one.* Dinky Stink laid those words like fly eggs in her ear. They hatched echoes. *You owe me one, one, one.* One what? Rita didn't think she had any of whatever it was to spare. Elbows, possibly. Knees? Nope, sorry. Can't pray. *Merde.* Why was Roger Christopher's French dribbling out of the mouth of that nun with the crooked habit and the cat's eyes? *Your guardian angel brought you this*, said Sister St. Anne, holding up a large paper cup. Chamuel sent me a milkshake and I don't even have a mouth to drink it with? Typical. But when Rita glanced into the cup she saw that it was full of ice, and embedded in the ice were two fingers, thumb and index, positioned in an AOK gesture. Or maybe it was sign language for something else. Knowing Chamuel, something obscene. Angelic innuendo, with its scuzzy underside. Also typical. She thought, I *must* have a mouth, because I'm laughing.

Live Bait

INNIS FLASHED DOWN a puzzle of roads like a Nasty Boy lure through water. Blue sky splashed over the hood, dust swirled up in his wake like silt. He was fleetness embodied, a flickering swiftness. A dash of silver in the eye. He flew up and down a maze of concessions, in and out of visibility, through bush, along rutted weed-knit tracks, past meadows and abandoned farms, down grassy undulate hills, *down*, in, away. He trolled and flaunted himself until the land struck hard, swallowed him deep, left him burning in its guts, its labyrinthine innards. *Lost*.

He flipped open the glove compartment to look for a map and a dead perch tumbled out. Did he ever forget directions? You kidding, he was sharp, he snapped them up and followed them to a T, correctly recasting the vague and imprecise ones, economically tightening the meandering thread of others. He got where he wanted to go because he *listened*, he followed the landmarks, the magnetic fields, the stars, and his own unerring instinct. But *what* had that guy at the garage said? *Turn rightleft rightleftrightrightrightnowaitit'sleftyeahleft thenright. Got that? Good, then you* ... Innis pinched the perch midstripe and shot it through the window like a dart. Dead bait. LaBelle Stink told him you had to show it a bit of action, dance it on the surface, if you wanted results. A live frog you can hook through the foreleg and he'll do the work for you, hopping like crazy. Just reel him back in and recast if he tries to sneak away and hide under some lily pad. A minnow you stab in the head, running the hook through its eyes, or through both lips if you want it to live longer. Worms are good in gobs, three or four nightwalkers speared in a No. 1 to 1/0 hook so there's lots of loose ends to wiggle and wave seductively at a largemouth in the market for a spirited snack. Some fish prefer grasshoppers, nymphs, larvae, doughballs, and a hunk of pork rind might win you a pickerel or pike long as a woman's leg. Innis hadn't realized that fish have such discriminating tastes and finicky palates, but LaBelle had set him straight on that, and a few other things besides.

He distinctly remembered *hang a right at Homer, near the Orange Hall, you can't miss it*. Though Ed or Gus, or whatever the guy's name was, had neglected to mention that the hall had been razed by fire twenty years ago, frying the squirrels in the attic and burning a hole the size of a dinner plate in Earl Peter's pants. The town was nothing more than a memory with an outhouse attached. The current population consisted of two citizens, Hera and Aphrodite, both shorthorns. Innis had grown wary of information willingly rendered by these people. Half the things they saw didn't even exist, at least not in the present moment. *Hear that?* It did it again. Surely *he* wasn't imagining things, phantom floating noises, his car gurgling and sloshing every time he navigated a curve or a hill. Like driving a bottle on a banking sea of roads, and he was the message tucked inside: s o s. But wait, he couldn't be lost. Lost was not in his itinerary. *Other* people dissolved into anonymity or flew apart like accidents whenever they hit the open road, but Innis was so intensely present that wherever he happened to be *was* the destination. Or so he felt. He was the elusive centre, the itinerant dot on the map. Significance travelled with him, glittering and sparkling on his skin like a matador's suit. If he were geography, he would be the terrain of desire, the place everyone wanted to be. *Olé!* Lost was for the muddled and sick and grieving and impoverished welter of humanity that lapped his shores, but couldn't touch him.

He gripped the wheel, sank his foot to the floor, and TOOK OFF! *Burble*. Burble? Did his Triumph TR4 actually make that vulgar sound? Whatever happened to *vroom* and *rrnnn*, those good old clichés of car diction? Funny, he used to understand his car. The bumps and knocks, the ticks and sproings weren't exactly brilliant conversation, but they conveyed meaning nonetheless – *fix this, adjust that*, plain and simple, and Innis would do it. Now the thing seemed to speak another language entirely, a fluid tongue as foreign to his ear as purling tumbling speech of rivers. Water jargon. And what had happened to the Inch archives in the trunk? How comforting it had been to hear them *clonk* and *bang* around in there as though it were old Inch himself pounding with his fists and slamming himself against the sides. After that submarine joyride in the channel, maybe the corpus had turned bellyup into a corpse, the papers and books swollen into silence, the text engorged with its own information and too bloated to budge. Imagine *years* of dry and dusty research – titillating for a Virgin specialist like Inch perhaps – but imagine it rinsed clean in the lake, leached off the page and translated into a work of substance, but a substance so shapeless and protean, impossible to grasp. Imagine that.

Glup? Only a car that was under some sort of molecular stress would say something like *glup*. A Triumph TR4 addressed the world with prevailing and conquering sounds. A Triumph TR4 was glory on wheels, it vanquished the road, riding it hard and close like a swift hand. It tooted its own horn, crowing *Veni, vidi, vici*. It was simply not in the mechanical nature of this vehicle to mimic a flush toilet. Or a jar of pickles. When Innis first heard its name, Triumph, how he loved it. It became him, he thought. *It's definitely you*, the salesman had said, and Innis had to agree. *Triumph* could easily be the title of his projected future autobiography, that sexy, sporty – and brief – document. The car was a flattering fit, snug and tight, displaying his physique to full advantage, filling in for his muscular blanks and other physical shortages, and the colour matched his hair, the imagined red. Or *did* match his hair until they painted it blue in the town garage. *Blue*.

'Yeah. So what's wrong with blue?'

'A few teeny minuscule scratches and you paint the whole bloody thing blue? I can't believe it.'

'Yeah. So what's wrong with blue?'

'My car is red, that's what's wrong. Red. Hot red, cherry red, fire engine red, hell and brimstone *red*.'

'Didn't have any.'

'My God, *blue!*'

'I got brown. Could redo'er in brown. But that'd be extra.'

'Man, I'll put it to you simply so you can understand it. Red is *fast*. Blue is not. Brown moves like shit.'

'That so? You in a big hurry?'

'Yesss.'

'Well then, here's your bill.'

Dredging and towing charges, parts and repair, *and* a paint job (it was *hardly* scratched), authored a bill that was at least a cubit long, but did that grease monkey fix the front axle, or check the suspension, or bleed the hydraulic brakes, or even replace the smashed headlight that was hanging loose as a popped eyeball? No wonder Innis was lost, his car groping along the road half-blind, a Cyclops with a bad case of indigestion. *Gorp!* Did you hear that? The guy didn't even dry it out properly, the seats were still damp, waterweeds festooned the grille. And the *smell*. His upholstery used to absolutely reek of money, a rich, leathery, freshly minted fragrance which he had tried to maintain and heighten with a product called New Car Odour that came in a spray can. Unfortunately, the spray had made it smell more like an economy family model Ford than a new Triumph. Better that, though, than this mossy mildewed decomposing stench that made him feel like he was at the wheel of a mobile catacomb, a dead man driving a crypt through the underworld.

Might as well be Hades, he thought, so far was he from intelligent life. Surely LaBelle Stink had been pulling his leg when she told him her family ate roadkill for supper. He had let her talk on and on, stringing him an interminable line of Stink stretchers. What *didn't* he know about those people, having been assailed with a superfluity of detail, all of it sub-significant, and yet each twisted particular so weird that it caught unforgettably in his mind like a cunningly crafted fly. Stink trivia, like a sudden inheritance that made him solvent in useless information. For instance, he would ever be cognizant of the fact that Burton preferred his pancakes all dressed, with ketchup, relish, onion rings, the works, and that Dolly dusts the house with her bare hands, a domestic molestation in which she slaps and smears and beats the dust into submission. That their daughter-in-law, Kim Stink, dies her pubic hair pink and keeps it trimmed in the shape of a valentine – genital topiary being, he supposed, the Stink version of arts and crafts. Beats macramé, anyway. That Chet Stink can play Jingle Bells and Have a Holly Jolly Christmas by bonking himself on the head with a wrench. *Never took lessons or nothin'*, LaBelle said of the family prodigy, who had apparently first discovered this unique talent when charging around the yard like a bull, head-butting his brothers and cousins, each assault producing a different but distinct musical note. And they all played 'wind' instruments, after supper on the porch ripping off flatulent riffs and trills and belching arpeggios. Outside of their cultural attainments, they enjoyed Stink sports, football played with an inflated pig's bladder, a water game involving a greased watermelon, and knife-throwing, usually at the back of the kitchen door, though any pliable surface would do, and they all had the scars to prove it.

And, 'What was that you just said?'

'We collect things.'

'Really? What sort of things?'

'Nothing much.' A strike! Now that she had him, she wasn't telling.

'I see.' Innis spat this out like a picky baleful pike skulking below the surface.

Okay, okay. 'Lightbulbs.'

'Hmmm?' A nibble.

'Tennessee Ernie collects lightbulbs.'

'What for?'

'What d'you mean *what for*? You stupid, or something? He's a collector. He collects lightbulbs.'

'Great. Interesting.' *Geez.* 'I suppose he has all kinds, does he?'

'Nope. Mostly hundred watters. Got about a thousand.'

'You mean he doesn't try to diversify his collection? Search out the tiniest bulb, say?' The merest seed of light. 'Or the most beautiful?' The Venus di Milo of lightbulbs. What a quest it would be, the first lightbulb ever, the mythical bulb cupped in his palm, an orb of translucent light. Fire stolen from the gods, borne in a beaker of glass.

'Why would he want to do that?'

'You said he was a collector.'

'Yeah, so?'

'Nevermind.'

Uh-huh, the barbed Stink smile. The old bat. She was a hoarder all right, you could tell, a rubber band saver if ever there was one. He wondered how many whitewall planters and bathtub grottoes decorated her front garden. The type usually found it pretty hard to restrict themselves to a mere one or two Virgin-filled and petunia-spewing samples. Collectors were a distinct breed, a digression taken on the evolutionary highway, a freakish strain of humankind that Innis followed at a safe, if attentive, distance, like a scavenging gull. He preferred to keep *things* in one category, and himself in another. None of this emotional bonding with material goods for him. (Not that he wasn't still annoyed over the loss of his phallic carving, an annoyance magnified by the shifty nature of that Holmes Stink, a man almost impossible to find.) Innis prided himself on his weight-lessness, his ability to drift free as an angel in a world where most people were mummified below a mountainous surfeit of stuff, encrusted with the disfiguring crud of all their possessions. The revenge of the inanimate. And the peculiar obsession of the collector, their bondage to the strangest of items, added to his contempt a fizzing spritz of wonder. Why *did* people ruin marriages, lose jobs, mortgage houses, wind up in jail, all in order to amass the world's largest collection of, say, toothpick holders? Or anvils? Or beer cans? Or photographs of one-armed midgets swimming the English Channel? Some lunatics collected fire trucks, or whole damn trains. Or even Edsels, with those daunting man-eating vaginal grilles. There was simply no telling when a reasonably sane and intelligent individual would one day wander into a flea market and be struck dumb by a doll with a tin head and bisque hands, a body made of rags. Rationality was a bridge off which a great many jumped with astonishing facility and abandon. Innis himself once went out with a woman who collected barbed wire, for the sole reason, she said, that her middle name was Barb. Her house reminded him of a cattle ranch, and he was the lone dogie, penned and imperilled, his shirts shredded and his wallet gaping at the staggering expense of those eighteen-inch sticks of E. S. Wheeler Spike Collar or Hart McGlin Star. Who would even take the time to name barbed wire, for cripes sake?

And of course his own drear unimaginative mother used to save string, odds and ends tied together and wound into a modest ping-pong sized ball. A harmless habit of domestic thrift that at some indefinable stage snowballed out of control, the thing growing to the size of a melon, then a basket ball, then an enormous waxing full moon that filled the kitchen and began sweeping objects into its orbit. He lost his socks, a bicycle clip, a bag of Halloween candy, and one time his dog Fritzy could be heard whining from within the ball's coiled depths.

His mother didn't notice. She stood transfixed before the monstrous reeled bulk, gratified and fulfilled by it in a way that neither marriage nor motherhood, religious devotion nor even shopping could match. More than an obstruction – it *was* damned hard to reach the toaster – it was to Innis a rival, a string sibling that he snipped at with manicure scissors on the sly. He buried firecrackers in it hoping to blow it apart, only to hear them softly implode like muffled farts. He keenly resented the fact that family life revolved around it, that it eclipsed the important events of his own young career, that he was made to stand beside it in photographs of his birthdays and graduation, more for scale than anything else. *My how it's grown*, people would say of it, not him. They never went on trips to the zoo or the museum, but to other towns to see other string balls. He had no idea how his mother knew that these existed – it was like going to search for UFOs and actually finding them. How incredible that there were other people like her in the world, busily splicing and knotting bits of string, twirling it lovingly in their fingers, winding and winding as though the activity had some purpose, as though they might eventually reel in some treasure, some revelation, however ineffable, at the end – and not just more string. *Mine's bigger*, his mother always concluded with a satisfied macho swagger as she swung her ample hips into their Volkswagen bug and beetled for home.

Not that he couldn't use that blasted ball now, something to unravel like a story to help find himself, or tell him at least if he was travelling in circles, charging up and down back roads that all looked the same to him. You'd have to be smitten with a particular stretch of rock and bush like this to be able to distinguish it from any other stretch of rock and bush. With a quick sweep of the eye in a jam-packed room in the complex heart of a city, Innis could readily pick out the salient (and saleable) details, identifying an ebonized Herter Brothers library table with its distinctive fieldmarks – the marquetry, the stylized golden chrysanthemums. He didn't necessarily want things, but he certainly *knew* them, could lavish on them affection-ate, almost concupiscent, attention, savouring the minutiae that told him clearly where he was (and how much he stood to make). But *here* the terrain rose up in his eye scabbed and tangled, a raw primary scribble in wood and stone, senseless, barren, land that only a Stink could love. (Never mind that it was the nursery of *Ranunculus repens* and *Veronicastrum virginicum*, floras far more exquisite and delicately detailed than any flower that had ever sprung from the Herter Brothers line.) Which is probably why he drove right past Stu Stink who was standing at the side of the road, one more undifferentiated lump in the landscape, a bonafide member of the scree. *Whoa! Was that a human being?* Innis squealed to a stop, then backed up into his own swirling skirt of dust.

When the motes settled, Stu emerged holding a sign on which was written in racked and misshapen letters the words *Live Bait*. An advertisement for which he apparently was the illustration, for he was covered in leeches, adorned and dashed with numerous slimy quivering black blobs. They were attached to his legs and arms, face and neck, and one even dangled from his earlobe like an earring made of hacked liver. He grinned gamely at Innis and waggled his eyebrows – you had to admire his commercial panache.

Innis rolled down his window. 'Creeping Jesus,' he said. 'Are you all right?'

'Yeah, sure. I stick 'em on and yank 'em off. Gives me somethin' to do. How many you want?' Stu started plucking the leeches, fondly pinching and tugging at them as though harvesting a crop of small external organs, which he then dropped one by one into a pail at his feet. *Plop. Plop*.

'Good *grief*, doesn't that hurt? Don't you feel faint?'

'Nah. The thing is not to put 'em in yer mouth, eh. Like, they could slip down and start suckin' on yer throat and they get swole up and you can't breathe and start chokin' and gaggin' and stuff. How many you want?'

'*None*. Thanks. I thought you might be able to give me a few directions. I'm trying to find the Stink farm.'

'How come?'

'I'm looking for something.'

'Is it long?'

'Yes, about four feet.'

'*Holy*. Is it hard?'

'Hard as rock.'

'Jumpin'! Does it got a head.'

'Two, actually.'

'*No shit?*'

'Say, you're a Stink, aren't you?'

How did he know *that*? Man, this guy was smooth. What could Stu say but, 'Yup.'

'Look, business is a bit slow, why don't I give you a ride home? Then you can show me the way. I'll even buy out your inventory. Leave it in the ditch there and I'll, ahh, pick it up later. How about it?'

'I dunno. Mum Stink said I shouldn't take rides with strangers.'

'Good advice.'

'She said they might try to steal me.'

'In your case, nooo, I don't think so.'

'Yer not gonna hurt me?'

'Honestly, I wouldn't know where to begin. Besides, I'm not a stranger. I know Granny. LaBelle? Your great-grandmother, I guess she'd be.'

'*Yeah?*'

'Sure. I met her in the hospital.'

'In the hospital? She still alive? Hell, we thought she croaked weeks ago. Whaddaya know. Wait'll I tell everybody.'

'Seriously? You mean to say you didn't know she was in the hospital?'

'Last I saw, she was smokin'. You know, we kinda wondered why there weren't no funeral.'

'Stu, did you say your name was?'

Did he say? Oooo, this guy was scary.

'Hop in, Stu.' Innis swung open the door on the passenger side and patted the seat, soft as a boy's cheek. 'Let me take you for a little ride.'

Ruthie woke up with a bee in her bonnet. A fly in her ointment. A black speck that homed in on her out of dark dreams and stuck in her eye, so she had to look over it, around it. Her irritation blossomed and bore fruit at a time-lapse gallop. *Her* turn to do the wash and the Stinks had all tied their socks together at the toes and pulled them tight. She broke her nails trying to unknot them. Why did they do this? To bug her, of course. Fine. She'd skip the rinse cycle, splash liberally with starch and hang their clothes on the line until they were as hard as boards, exaggerated and indelible clothes-peg-pinch biting into the bottom corners of their shirts – a Stink identifier if there ever was one. By the time she was through they'd all be waddling and tottering around stiff as a deck of cards. Which is what they were.

Baby Stink was cranky, too, taking his cue from her. *Don't*, she'd warned, meaning the worm that Gram had given him to play with, which he was about to taste-test. Baby stuck out his bottom lip and said, distinctly, as though he'd been born with the word in his mouth and only now decided to spit it out, 'Bitch.' What?! *Bitch?* Her? His *dear* mother? Ten words in his vocabulary, *ten*, and how many of them were already blighted, fouled? She knew there'd be no getting rid of it, either, no purging it with soap and water. Swear words stained worse than blood and wouldn't wash. Stu and Dinky and all those other Stink brats had eaten so much soap in their formative years that they had acquired a taste for it. Every frigging bar of Lifebuoy in the house had teeth marks in it and chunks missing. No, Baby Stink clearly owned the word now and she wouldn't be able to wrest it out of his chubby grip as she would a shard of glass or any other dangerous object. It stood between them, and others would surely follow, a blizzard of words – *cow, bag, witch, whore* – strong enough to blow her straight across the room, maybe right out the door. And what could she ever say to him that would be of any help, that would mend the breach? *Wipe your nose, do up your coat, don't play on the road, don't talk to strangers, listen, be careful, listen to me*, were just words, useless, feckless words with no muscle, like thin arms made of air through which he'd tumble into disease and crime and other Stink hobbies. Oh, bad bad mood.

Lay off the kid, Gram had said that morning, implying that she was crushing him with her attentions, the rock-solid weight of her love. And, *Say Nits, why doncha get a hairdo like Kim's?* He wasn't talking about the fuzzy orange stuff growing on the top of Kim Stink's head, either. Pig. Thorn in her side. Grit in her bed. How was it that lately Gram had become one more abrading Stink irritant? How had he resolved his gorgeous accommodating body into a form so small and sharp, painful as a stuck bone or tack? How exactly does a man become the rash between your toes, the cracker crumbs in your nylons? He opens his mouth, that's how. He lets the blackflies out, the sawdust, the greasy spores and slivery fibres that comprise his minuscule hardly-to-be-credited intelligence. Stuff that in your blowhole, eh, big boy. Ruthie whipped a pot off the table and kicked it clear across the room, splattering last night's supper on the walls. A tickling flyaway wisp of hair drifted into her face and she smacked it savagely away. She glared at Baby Stink, radiating so much psychic electricity that he felt it bore like a drill into his pudgy cheek and he screamed in terror. The phone was ringing and ringing. Either it was Liz calling to jabber hysterically about that Rita Cabal kid – dead or alive, who cares? – or it was her mother, weepy and contrite, desperate to bounce the softly spun ball of her voice against Ruthie's stubbornly held silence. *Fuck it*. (Actually, Grace Stronghill hadn't quite gotten around to placing that call, apologizing for publicly insulting her daughter, which made Ruthie livid, even more determined that she would never yield to those crooning corrupting words when they were finally delivered like a rotting bouquet to her door.) *Fuck it all to hell. Smash*, Ruthie thought, *rip, tear.* She envisioned a neck in her hands which broke with a clean satisfying *snap!* She ground her teeth. An annoying *rat-scratching tap-tapping* at the door snagged her attention and she whirled over to it and booted it open. A man stood before her, vaguely familiar, a tentative wavering smile playing upon his lips. She grabbed him by the shirt front, yanked him in and slammed the door, then began undressing him, roughly yet thoroughly, shucking him clean as a cob of corn. Naked as a noodle.

'Hey, I remember *you*,' she said, looking him over, then staring down in undisguised amusement. 'My, my. *What* a surprise.'

These weren't the last words Innis heard before drowning in the stinging voluptuous sea that instantly overwhelmed him, that plunged him headfirst into the cold immediate quick of what he thought must be life itself, its very pulse, unsheathed, and beating so thrillingly against him.

'Lookit here, Chet,' a voice drifted in from somewhere outside, raucous as a crow's cry, 'Ed left half a bottle of rye sittin in this guy's engine. The old boozer.'

Before he succumbed entirely, filling his lungs to the full in this astonishing element, letting it slide like silk down his throat, a slick watery garment pouring into his veins, he heard someone else yell, 'Roadkill.' This announcement was accompanied by a kind of hooting war cry, and the sounds of people clamouring, running, joyous, vigorously beating up the dust with their feet, arms flung wide – or so he imagined – as if rushing to embrace distance itself and desire incarnate.

Mary's Dress

LIKE DARK ANGELS performing somersaults, the gloaming tumbled softly through the windows of the Church, did a slow handspring up the aisle and into the altar, past Victor Cabal, saint's physician, who was kneeling at the altar rail, praying so hard, clasping his hands so tightly together, it's a wonder he didn't break his wrists. The concentration of prayer had isolated in his mind a floating remnant of cloth. Immaterial material. Blue, naturally. Colour of the impossible. A petal of unutterably delicate fabric suspended and held fluttering on a steady updraft of faith.

In the seventh century, Greek soldiers – plundering? raping? – discovered the Virgin Mary's dress concealed in a golden reliquary. This find itself was like a golden key which unlocked her closet doors, soon to be thrown wide open. A virtuous and undemonstrative woman with hardly a thing to wear was suddenly revealed to be in possession of a voluminous wardrobe, including racks of fabulously embroidered medieval gowns, veils, grave clothes (Assumption notwithstanding), silky intimate apparel, and girdles splattered with drops of breast milk. Even the shift she wore at the Annunciation turned up like a trump card. Given the extent of the articles amazingly produced, pulled out of ecclesiastical sleeves, it would seem she found more bargains in her day than Blondie and that she had the habits of a teenager, letting her clothes lie wherever she dropped them, scattered over most of Europe. Churches almost everywhere housed sartorial relics to which one could crawl on one's knees for help. The merest thread of Mary's clothing, blue as a vein, was a direct line of communication. A tangible language, she could be thanked in kind, as in that little church in Italy where women bring their wedding dresses and offer them to Mary for favours rendered, hundreds of them, piles, paragraphs of lace and satin gratitude for the blessing of potent husbands and bouncing babies. But in this matter-of-fact country, Victor lamented, its climate hostile to miraculous occurrence, women made curtains out of their wedding dresses, or entombed them in trunks, keeping out the light. Here, the communal imagination was weak, flying saucers about the best it could come up with. Well, let the rationalists jeer, like his brother, rationalized to the bone. They missed the point. Was not credulity a gift, a talent, and was not belief a discipline? And believers at times needed talismans, these spiritually impregnated costumes and props, for they were the portals that opened on the inaccessible. Any relic, poetically authentic at least, was a stone door rolled aside, a passage down which one could whisper into the ear of the Almighty. And if He wouldn't listen, you addressed those who would intercede on your behalf. Like Mary. She was a woman. She always listened.

So Victor was keeping his mind's eye on a conjured shred of Mary's dress, knowing ... no, *believing* his daughter's life depended on it. Dr Nopper had given him and his weeping Sofia such a despairing look before Rita was wheeled into the operating room, a pail of leeches tucked under his arm. Leeches! This did not inspire confidence. If a medical doctor had to resort to primitive technique, who dared call his creed and fervent effort superstition? *Don't tell me you still believe in that childish crap*, his brother had said, and maybe he was right. Victor *was* a child, Mary's child, as all men were. And if so, he intended to hold onto the tag end of her dress persistently as any child and *not let go* until he got what he wanted. His clutching fist would be the puckering burr in her sacred raiments. Only a miracle would shake it loose. Why take chances with his precious daughter? A miracle herself, so long had he and Sofia waited for her. Years of searching fruitlessly for her in their huge marriage bed – was she hiding under a pillow, lost in the creases? Victor was not about to entrust Rita's already hardwon life to fumbling human hands. *Hail Mary, full of grace* ... Mary was all-merciful, loving, soft as her flowing gown, and a parent herself, she would not allow anyone to take his child from him. He would promise anything. He would *die* for Rita, diving through his wounds directly into the boiling pitch of hell. A religion of wounds, that's what his brother had called it, a weird cult obsessed with the body, with mortified flesh, corporal resurrection, torture, crucifixion, cannibalism, *this* is my body, *this* is my blood. So, and his brother wasn't obsessed with the body? Victor had crept like a thug into his own workroom, taking a hammer to St. Anthony's fingers, knocking them off one by one, hostages now in his suitcoat pocket, which he patted with a grim satisfaction. Never hurt to have a little extra insurance. Besides, under the Church's ornate theatrical vestments, it *was* a visceral religion, and he wanted to make sure they were all speaking the same language.

Really now. After the Annunciation, you'd think women would be wary of windows, of sitting by them as they sipped their tea, letting the sun pour its pagan gold over their bare knees and slippered feet, the shadow of some enormous bird descending. Burnt once already, you'd think that Liz Stronghill would know better. Her mother, muttering and gesticulating, hustled off to fetch Liz a robe. (Says Grace to herself, 'You don't mean to tell me she worked all day like *that?*) Liz sat by the kitchen window, slip askew and straps fallen, a bug stuck in her lipstick. She was staring down into her empty teacup. The moment was ripe for the certainty of some calamity to sink its talons into the side of her head and *tap tap tapping* with the ferocity of a grub-crazed woodpecker, break into her brain. If not a winged messenger, then perhaps a paranormal assault. Or simply intuition, the complex circuitry that connects mother and child, lighting up and sending her a jolting shock. *Rita*, she whispered, dropping the cup, which shattered on the floor along with the unread future it contained.

Early theologians believed that Mary conceived through her ear – *quod aure virgo concepit* – virgin eardrum intact. A gentle enough siring on the Lord's part, easy as an idea, considering the consequences. An act executed certainly with more delicacy than some of Zeus's sexual shenanigans. Blake Hardy had about as much biological information at his fingertips, and yet, like Mary giving her ear to the Holy Spirit, they managed nonetheless. Seated by the same kitchen window, a decade or so ago, following a nightlong vigil and council with the shadows, Liz was apprised of two stone cold facts: Blake was dead, and she was pregnant. While he had been tossed into the air and scattered like a handful of petals – *he loves me, he loves me not* – she had discovered herself to be, well, pollinated. She just *knew it*, Gabriel couldn't have put it more succinctly. Blake had put it succinctly enough, leaving Liz that little souvenir of himself, that fertile relic, before being swallowed up by the dark – no prophetic confidences swishing like a luminous drink in *his* ear. What remained on this earth of his living substance he had deposited for safekeeping *in* her, a tiny flame about to flare up and consume her. Widow kindling chucked on his funeral pyre, her life as good as gone. What could she do? What choice did she have, stuck in this particular time and place? She didn't live so long ago that she was required to drown herself in the lake. Nor yet so very long ago that Mary herself would personally intervene, her sense of loyalty to supplicating sinners far outweighing considerations of earthly morality. Oh, to be in a medieval miracle play, where a romping cussing mother of God would whisk in to save the day. But no, you can't deprive people of their pound of flesh. Unless you're a Stink and simply don't care. Stinks breed like rabbits anyway, and its hard to tell which kids belong to which sets of parents. Her parents had a *name* to uphold. Good God, what *would* they say, she remembers thinking. That is, after the heart attacks and ritual hair pulling. *Dear, you know you can't keep it, we couldn't possibly, you have your future to consider.* ... Shame has its conventions, and its conventional punishments. She went away 'to school' for a year, got rid of it quietly. If she pretended to forget, everyone in town pretended not to know, all the while *knowing* gave them a particular keen pleasure, and her not forgetting gave her an especially keen pain. Like having the skin ripped off her hands was how it had felt giving her baby away. Her baby. Away. End of story. Goodnight.

But wait, wait. There's a twist, a thickening in the plot like a cancerous lump. Get this. Who should move to town but a Portuguese couple with a new baby, an adopted baby. None other than. *What a co-inky-dinky,* Chet Stink might say, collisions being his specialty. Or, *That's life!*

Liz would not have called her daughter Rita, a tough name she worked in her mouth like a piece of gristle. Gabriella, maybe. Michelle. Or Mary, Maria ... *full of grace.* How do you mother out of the corner of your eye, muzzled, hands tied behind your back? She had stood under Rita's window at night with prayer caught like a bit in her teeth. She had embraced the Cabal house itself and received its cold gritty kiss. Impetuously, *foolishly,* she had even climbed up the trellis and into Rita's room. She stood in the corner watching her sleep, terrified of the distance between them, knowing she could never fling her arms open wide enough to gather her in. Her baby. And now *this.* This divine intelligence, the teacup smashed, like father like daughter. No news is good news. Truly, when you see an angel sweeping down, goat eyes bright as golden coins, let alarm fill you with its driving breath, and *run.* Run for your life.

For her part, Sister St. Anne couldn't honestly tell anymore whether she was the Bride of Christ or the Bride of Frankenstein. The groom had taken to his heels, leaving her *at large*, a bride in trouble, seriously knocked up and about to give birth at any moment through her mouth. For days she wandered around with an undigested fist in her stomach, a whole head lodged in her chest. Her nostrils and ears were plugged with fingers and toes, skin dropped from beneath her lids like curtains and clung to her eyeballs. Long hair trailed down the inside of her legs, tickling unbearably. Whatever was trapped inside her rubbed and chafed, kicked and bit, gnawing at her, sending her whirling around the room. She ripped her missal in two with her bare hands. She broke into the hospital pharmacy and downed half a bottle of red liquid marked *Prussic Acid*, pouring the rest into the kitchen soup pot. She roared into the chapel and put her foot through a stained-glass window, taking the legs off St. Joseph, then punched out the Holy Child in his arms, exploding Him like a bomb. She stuck her finger down her throat and retched into the font, though all that came out was a ragged veil, a pink swaddling cloth long and fluid, but empty as a lung.

Parts of the Flower

IN THIS CEILING-HIGH suspension of disbelief, the Holy Ghost, say, is stationed like a surveillance camera in the corner of the room. Perhaps roosting on the stuffed moosehead, or on the mounted and shellacked Northern pike caught by William B. Hawk in 1943 and donated on his passing to this, his favourite watering hole, by his generous and joyful widow. The Holy Ghost doesn't usually hang out in bars, but they too are sanctuaries housing the spiritually involved. Take that man seated by the door, a stranger with wraith-white hands who holds a newspaper up in front of his face. Given its banner, *Jornal do Incrível,* it might have been published in heaven. Translated, some of its headlines read: *A Miracle! Child's Life Saved by Leeches* or *Confirmed Midget Grows Inch* or *Statue of St. Anthony Weeps Real Tears* or *Nun Drinks Blood, Goes Berserk* or *Leg Gnawed off Man by Ravenous Baby.* Obviously, the air here is thick with more than smoke, and this modest room is yet large enough for the incredible to stretch and unfurl its wings. Saturated with anecdote and gossip, it is intoxicatingly rich, voluble as any sanctified space. Even the ratty burn-pocked tables and chairs have tales to tell, lies grow like grout in the cracks. That pike on the wall could easily swim again immersed in its own fish story, the fiction of its capture kept alive here and filtering through its gills as pure as verbal oxygen. Or the moose might come crashing out of the wall through a thicket of invention, searching for that one fatal word-borne bullet. Stories wash through the room, whisky-soaked and spring-fed, well-deep or skimmed off the glittering surface of the lake, long and twisty as rivers, brief and self-centred as puddles. They are salvaged from family histories, hearsay, make-believe, and drawn out of nowhere like sudden dunning love.

Remember the *Norgoma's* beautiful whistle, someone says, deep-toned and steamy? Remember the boat that foundered during the great storm but didn't sink because it was carrying a cargo of oranges? Thousands of buoyant sunny globes keeping it afloat. Everyone thought it was haunted. Captain Mackie went down with his ship. Yeah, but only after he was criticized for not going down with the first one that sank. They say that drowning's addictive.

That's screwy. If you've come close once, you'll go back again and again. What if you were on a doomed ship and you had only a minute left to live, what would you do with it? Puke. I'd write a message on the door, *Goodbye, Winnie. I never meant any harm. All my love, Bertie.* Would you put in the punctuation? I'd *be* the punctuation. My grandfather cured his ellipses by drinking well water out of a skull. Don't you mean epilepsy? My grandmother had a head of red hair so long that she wrapped it around her chest in the winter for warmth. You mean to say she wore a hair shirt, har har? When my mother was a girl in the old country a man was murdered in her village and his head was hacked off and thrown down the well and thereafter the water ran sweet half the year and bitter as gall the rest. Bullshit. When I was in the war I heard tell of a soldier whose head was severed, sliced off clean with a bayonet, but the head still spoke. What in God's name did it say? Cursed a bloody blue streak, what d'you think? Those wild Irish boys. Remember that dance in the town hall in Homer when Pat Shea, on a bet, jumped barefoot over five salt barrels laid side by side and had to walk home in the snow minus his big toenail and his rooster? Sure, but he stole the rooster back the next night. Who set that fire? You should know. Farquhar's had a fire sale that lasted eight years. Whatever happened to that birdbath the Sheas used to have in their garden? You know, that funny squatty thing made of stone? A man it was, two men actually, back to back, and two heads, with a kind of basin scooped out at the top. Hell if I know. Remember that archaeologist guy who *sat* on a quartzite flake? *Big* discovery. Hey Roger, how about another round here, that's r-o-u-n-d.

A slow pan, dove-eyed and omniscient, from the talkers to the bartender reveals a familiar, if unexpected, figure. French lace, snakeskin shoes, fishnet stockings ... who else but Roger Christopher, the separate school teacher, moonlighting, working the nightshift in this institution of higher learning. You can bet no one staggers out of the Ocean House bar totally swacked or stoned stupid. Rather, with hundred-proof education under their belt they'd be bibulous or pixillated, clutching a degree on a rolled-up napkin, a report card scribbled on a coaster. Roger Christopher set certain standards. What other town drunk anywhere could rattle off the names of the fur traders, the inventor of the steam engine, the capitals of all the countries in the world, their imports and exports? *Corn*, announces

Gilbert Aelicks, snoozing on the gentle desk his arms make, when someone pokes him. Knowledge pops out of his mouth like gold coins. And the rule is here, if you can't spell a drink, you can't have it.

'Gimme a r-u-m c-o-c-k-t-a-l-e.'

'Tsk, only half right, Fred. You can have the mix.'

'How about a m-a-r-t-i-n-y, then?'

'Empty glass, Fred.'

'Okay, so I'll settle for a straight j-i-n.'

'Lost your glass, Fred. Here, you want djinn, read some Kipling. There'll be a test in half an hour.'

The bar was as well stocked with books as it was with booze. The finest ports and brandies occupied shelf space with the greatest literature, while the plonk was filed with the commercial trash. The order of a Black Russian inevitably came with a volume of Tolstoy, a Rob Roy brought Sir Walter Scott, an Old Fashioned, Thomas Hardy, and a Bloody Mary, a little something by Mary Lamb. No one ever ordered a Scarlett O'Hara, nor a drink called a Ward 8 lest they get something incomprehensibly modern and depressing. For the beer drinkers there were primary readers. What a congenial atmosphere it was, in which imbiber and bibliophile could meet as one. Lubricated insights and epiphanies went off around the room like flashbulbs. New light was shed on old work, understanding was deepened and expanded. For the most part, that is. Should Roger Christopher notice someone slapping his thighs and cracking up over *Being and Nothingness*, he'd cut him off, give him a bookmark, and send him outside for some fresh air.

When Holmes Stink ordered the usual, he received a double Scotch and a bulky word-sodden dictionary, which he clasped manfully to his chest as he wandered to his table in the corner under the moosehead. Even a spiritual spy would have to shift position, cock an eye, regard him at an unusual angle, this fellow with water in his ears and a bouquet of flowers stuck in his head. Not literally of course, he's thinking about columbine, the roots of the word, the delicate pinkish-yellow columbary its flower makes. A dovecote. Holmes's problem is that he spells too well, a spelling bee representing to him an opportunity to probe the flowery flesh of a word for its treasure, its saffron dust. And – with his finger he makes a whirlpool in his glass of Scotch then drinks the swirl of it down – liquid is his natural element. For days in the hospital when Rita drifted in and out, Holmes drank so much that he practically swam to her, his sharp breath sending a ripple of recognition over her face, still as a plaster saint's. Of all the antidotes applied to Rita, her father's prayers and mother's tears, even the doctor's leeches that swilled the unwanted blood pooling in her reattached fingers, she credited Holmes with saving her life, calling her back, finding her among the flotsam of her broken and scattered self. The healing salve of his presence by her bed, his hand a canopy of warmth over her own damaged one. The glinting restorative wink of his silver flask as he raised it to his lips. His words, staggering a little, stumbling as they tried to walk a straight line out of his mouth. His own form of magic medicine he urged her to swallow. *Say luminous, Rita. Lustral. Libation.* Another drink. *Say window. Wind's eye.* Listening, Rita saw herself stepping carefully from one floating plank of wreckage to the next, getting closer and closer to the shore. *He* was her guardian angel, turning sharply away and snapping his fingers, deflating her predatory phantom of an uncle, making him collapse like steam into a bed pan, warm piss carried out by an orderly. Could Holmes actually *see* what she did? Unlike her parents, who saw only him, a grown man at her bedside, a drunk *and* a Stink. How they resented and distrusted him, clearly infatuated with their young daughter, it wasn't right. Any parent would feel the same. They complained and had him thrown out of her room, so he went to the Ocean House for a drink. D-a-i-q-u-i-r-i. Most people can't even say it. *I almost went under, too,* he told Rita later. *That's the buddy system for you.*

A ray of light shed through the dead fur and dusty antlered aura of the moosehead would reveal that Holmes had arrived at the W's. Wi … wit … what was it about Rita's family that bothered him? Most children are afraid of the dark, but only the injured ones, the ones with some black secret buried savagely in them, take the dark in their own hands and make of it something so wholly convincing. Headless men in closets. Fear all dressed. *There*, he's found it, finger touching the very word, underlining and warming it, *wittold*.

At the bar a lesson is in progress.

'Hey, sure I know the answer. That's easy. The labia, the hymen, umm, the cervix.'

'I said parts of *the* flower, Stuart, not *de*flower. Sit down, please. Now who can name …'

The man with the pale white hands is gone, leaving behind his newspaper crumpled on the table, along with his half-finished drink, an Angel's Kiss, the glass weeping wet haloes on a copy of *Paradise Lost*. The door creaks open and another stranger appears, a slice of his face visible through the crack. He opens the door further, enough to step in, tentatively, as though testing the temperature of the water, the toe of his black shoe probing like a dog's nose. That which you might say is fluid here instantly evaporates. Books vanish into pockets, all conversation stops. Story is only so much dried spit on the floor. The intruder, Innis George, glances around, eyes blinking. This could be any rural bar, given the campy hunting and fishing trophies on the wall, and, up in the corner there, *Jesus*, he thinks, *did someone actually kill and stuff a dove? Barbarians*. And true, the clientele wears the usual moronic look, regulation lumberjack shirts and Co-op caps, corn ascendant on the crests. Innis sticks out his chin and brazens the open stares, managing a dignified if somewhat self-conscious swagger toward the bar. He swings his leg over the barstool. Hell, these dudes want to talk barbed wire, he's your man.

'What'll you have?' Roger Christopher wipes a glass with the hem of his dress.

'A Shirley Temple,' someone mutters from behind.

'How about a Ruthie Stink?' someone else suggests, and the room fills with wheezy sly laughter like a den full of amused serpents.

Innis stares a long moment at Roger Christopher, before finally asking, 'Why are you wearing that dress?'

How blunt.

'Better than wearing nothing at all.'

My, but word travels fast. Innis had travelled even faster when Gram broke through the kitchen door – he *could* have opened it, it wasn't locked – and Ruthie said, *You're dead meat now, I guess*. Funny how much quicker you can move without clothing, skinny dipping in sheer terror.

'Stamens,' says Gilbert Aelicks, exporting images from a distant dream country.

Stone-faced Gram. Innis was amazed at how much he resembled those pictures of grotesques he'd encountered in Inch's papers – distorted grimacing faces, massive tongues hanging down to their chins. Ruthie, on the other hand, was definitely not grotesque. Not stone. Inner thighs, soft as petals. Breasts.

'You should take stock,' advises Roger Christopher, setting a drink before him.

'Stock?'

'Missing inventory. Let's see, so far you've lost your phallic carving, Dr Inch's research material, your marbles (temporarily), your pants, those blue socks with the hole in the toe, and a pair of jockey underwear, size small.'

'How on earth do you know all this?'

'I'm the teacher. Eyes in the back of my head. Don't even think of making a spitball. You'll only lose it.'

'But –'

'Frank, tell us, which do women find sexier, jockey underwear or boxer shorts?'

'Umm, I'd have to say boxers, Roger. Especially if they're wrinkled and catch in your rear, that drives a woman wild, no telling what she'll do.'

'You might want to bear this in mind, Innis.'

'Who *are* you? And look, *look* in the bottom of my glass, what *is* that?'

'Spaghetti.'

'What?'

'As is the olive to the martini, the beauty spot to the cheek, the hyphen to the compound modifier, so too is the piece of spaghetti to the iceworm cocktail. Frank, what have you done with the Robert Service?'

'Damn, I left it in the can.'

'If you want Service, I'm afraid you'll have to get it in the washroom.'

'Fine. I was going there anyway.' *Jee-zus*, he could only take these people in small doses. They were like shots of moonshine, jiggers of hundred-proof madness. With luck there'd be a window in the bathroom he could climb through. To hell with finding that goddamn elusive Holmes Stink. (So *that's* why Holmes has been sitting with his hands held up in front of his face, studying his palms like an open book, impossible to put down.) Living by the water must take its toll, he decided, all that moisture rusting out the mental machinery. He wondered how far past the shoreline the lake extended its influence – obviously they were all in over their heads without knowing it. Even to him, this egress through windows was beginning to feel as natural as it would to a diver slipping through the window of an underwater wreck. Why go through a door (especially if some big goof like Gram is blocking the way)? Doors are for the narrow-minded and gravity-footed. Take these washroom doors, for instance. Products of a simple, single-syllable culture. *Milt*, said one. *Roe*, the other. What? Milt? Roe?

The sexual designation of a door was not normally a problem for Innis. No matter how ostentatiously knobbed, the identifying information was usually quite reliable. In his experience, if a door had anything at all to declare about its sexual orientation, it did so unequivocally and tersely, in a word or two (which is more than you can say for some people). What it had to say might be coy or silly, as in 'Cowgirls' and 'Buckaroos', but as long as you knew the idiom in which you needed to relieve yourself, then *entrez* and negotiate your business in the privacy of your own gender. But, Roe? And, Milt? Milt was a man's name, of course. But then, roe had about it a masculine sense of thrust and drive, as in *roe, roe, roe your* –

'See that?'

'Sure, he went into the ladies. You surprised?'

'I don't mean *him*, Casanova there.'

'More like Casserole. That boy's all mixed up.'

'You mean Holmes? Yeah, he cleared that table. Didn't think a Stink could move that fast.'

'No, not Holmes. You telling me you didn't *see* it?'

'See what, for cripes sake?'

'That weird light that just swept through the room. Up near the ceiling. Looked like some sort of bird. But really bright. Like white fire.'

'Guano,' mutters Gilbert Aelicks.

'Whoa, Stan, I think you've had too much to read.'

Go. Scat. Exit skyward, spiralling up and up.

Should the Holy Ghost take a final look at the earth and the earth-bound, it would see a man hurling himself into the channel as if defying those very bonds, breaking into the lake with such urgency that he leaves his thoughts floating behind on the surface like a scattered bouquet of wild flowers. And in the Ocean House directly below, another man is stuck in a small window, arms waving desperately, hands clawing at the air like someone drowning in a confusion of elements. Not much in the way of intelligence to report, this secret agent might just conclude as an updraft soft as a sigh carries it heavenward. Who would believe it anyway?

Speak of the Devil

THINK OF A PAINTING, Renaissance, two angels flat out, bed clothes undulate as flowing robes around them, scrolled messages in Gothic script unfurling out of their mouths like antique speech balloons. 'What the hell,' says the elder of the angelic creatures. 'Weird,' says the other much younger one, pulling the message like a stretchy band of mozzarella out from between her teeth. 'What does yours say, Granny?'

'Hard to tell. I wasn't finished lunch when I took that damn pill.'

'Mine says, *Glory be to God for dappled things.*'

'Mine's dappled, that's for sure.'

'What do you think it means?'

'That we both got fortune cookie messages in our penicillin capsules? It means somebody in this damn hospital is off his nut. Wonder how much of this garbage I've already swallowed? Get this.' Granny wiped off the strip of paper with her sheet. '*You will meet a short, dark, overweight stranger with horns.* Sounds like our goat, Nick. Say, I'm really lookin' forward to that, eh.'

'Maybe it's some kind of medical experiment. Like they're trying to cure us with words, with different sayings and stuff.'

'That's us, two rats in a maze.' LaBelle tamped her message into a ball and flicked it off her thumb into Rita's water glass. 'Bingo!'

Granny enjoyed showing off her digital dexterity, but it didn't bother Rita. Her own flicking fingers were still knitting themselves back onto her hand, getting reacquainted, reborn blood vessels snouting through deep flesh like rootlets. Her hand, so stiff and seamed. Strange to her. Often, she would hold it up to study this otherness grafted onto her. When her torn fingers had returned, they no longer seemed the same, no longer seemed to be hers, and they brought back with them, corralled in their small imperfect circumference, something she didn't have before. A gift. Or call it a power. Something, anyway, with the heft of thickened air, or light, a fullness not quite visible. Dr Nopper's leeches had fed on this as much as on the excess blood pooling in her fingers, rolling off in a satiated swoon, fat as cigars. She had healed in excess of everyone's expectations. Even her imaginary wounds were gone. The plumbing in her palms, the stigmata that had slaked down like drains whatever happiness she had ever managed to catch hold of. She could bury her face in her hands now and they smelled like flowers.

'Wrists,' said LaBelle. 'You know, eh, they nailed Him through the wrists. Otherwise He woulda ripped and slid off.'

Random observations rolled out of Granny's head like loose change, catching in the sunlight as they wobbled past. Or she might pull out a bulky wad of anecdote and peel off some generous autobiographical denomination, spendthrift with her life. She might throw it all up in the air, making you snatch and grab for it, a wealth of experience waterfalling down. A rain of gems. Undoubtedly treasure, though, and worth scrabbling for, Rita knew that.

'When I was a girl, they turned the school around.'

'The building?'

'Twelve men, all farmers of course, strong as bulls, shoulders wide as shacks, came one day and hoisted 'er around, south to north.'

'With the students in it?'

'Sure. Alls we had to do was turn our desks the other way.'

'But why? What for?'

'For the light, what d'you think? It was all over us. Poured into our hands like honey. We saw everything different then.'

And, because she was a Stink, wildlife crept in. The birds and the bees. The way LaBelle told it, Rita felt the peck and the sting.

'Do you believe in the Devil, Granny?'

'Believe in him? I *married* him.'

'Grampa Stink?'

'Bad as they come.'

'Really?'

'Bad *bad*. Didn't want to get married, diddled both my sisters, tryin' to squirm out of it. You know diddled?'

'I think so?'

'You done it?'

'Come on, Granny, I'm only a kid.'

'Zella was only twelve. Hattie, fourteen. I think every damn female at my wedding was knocked up by the groom. And he pissed in my hat.'

'Your wedding hat?'

'Punched it clean off my head. Said it looked like a pisspot. Then you better sit in it I said cause you're a shit. This, right before the wedding.'

'Did you cry?'

'You serious? I climbed a tree out back of the church where I seen this bird's nest, all wove with bark and twigs and butts, and even a sprig of forget-me-nots, *in bloom*, and I got it down and wore that. It was real pretty.'

'I bet you were beautiful, Granny. But I don't understand why you wanted to marry him. You know, if he was so mean to you.'

'He *was* mean, and dirty. Ran around. Drank. Fought.'

'So ... *why* did you?'

'Like you said, you're just a kid. Hear that? Thunder. And I'm stuck in this hell hole with half my skin hanging off. Lightning fried Aunt Mavis. Come right through the window and run up her iron bed, her grabbing one a the posts in her sleep. (Wonder *what* she was dreaming about?) Storm come up and mother would hightail it to the closet, newspaper over her head. Not me. I hear the sky crack open and I'm gone like a shot. I used to rip my clothes off and run out the kitchen door. Weren't happy till I had rain on my tongue runnin' down my throat. Rain so hard it hurts.'

Rita pondered this, being accustomed to information tucked inside verbal envelopes, delivered in parables.

'Remember that time he was building the shed. August. It was hot. Thought I'd take him a nice cold beer. I walked round the corner of the house, swingin' the bottle by the neck, whistlin' some little ditty I near choked on when I caught sight of him. Did he look *good*, shirt off, all shiny with sweat. Big chest. Mmph. I couldn't stand it. I could feel this kiss squeezing up my lips like frog-talk. I started to run, and that's when he saw me. Coming at him full speed ahead. He looked kinda scared. Eyes got all big. You see, I didn't realize his mouth was full a nails. Shit, he musta swallowed half a dozen. Got blood all over my face. And the beer ran right down the crack in his arse. Heh.'

'I guess you really love him?'

'Hell no, bugger makes me gag.'

'Back then, though?'

'Mmm. Hey, want to come to a party?'

'Okay, sure. When?'

'Zzzzzzzz.'

Rita raised herself up to look, and yes, Granny had fallen instantly, head over heels, into sleep. She was the only person Rita knew who actually said *zzzzzzz*, a quick conversational getaway, the sound of her roaring off, tearing into this altered state with the vigour of a buzzsaw, felling whole stands of dreams. In LaBelle's case this sudden dropoff into sleep wasn't so much a failing of age, as habit. A lifetime of Stink dodges, of flight, of chasing and consorting with storms, had given her the social graces of a hit-and-run driver. She left you with the climax of your sentence crumbling in your mouth, the dregs of it running down your chin. She hears the school bell ringing, or the sky exploding like fireworks in some other part of her life, and she's gone. But she'd be back, emerging out of sleep wearing a wisp of a smile like a woman stepping out of a secret room. Then Rita could find out more about the party, if nothing else about love, which seemed to have a lot to do with men's shoulders. Like most Stinks, LaBelle circled the subject warily, as if it were poisoned meat. Their tongues adroitly avoided the very word, taking crude and rutted detours around it, travelling anywhere but. Stu, for instance, who had this crush on Rita but no language for what he was feeling, so love ran out of his fists into the round freckled faces of young children and other sundry receptacles of Stink emotion. Even Holmes, when Rita queried him, narrowed his eyes protectively, keeping unwanted visions out.

'Don't you have a girlfriend, Holmes?'

'Girlfriend? Girlfriend ...' he said, thumbing mentally through his inventory of lost and found objects. 'No-o-o, but I once had a pet heron. Named her Beth. Did I ever tell you about Beth? Now, *she* was cute.'

Rita sighed, and rolled her eyes. Never mind, she had plans for Holmes, and the power in her hands now to execute them. This overreaching the limits of her own life had worked wonders, annealing and tempering them for difficult, indeed impossible, tasks. When Granny fired herself off to sleep, licking across the surface of her time spent, Rita raised her hands before her – *this is the church, this is the steeple* – and prayed. Her two small hands, clasped together and pointing at the ceiling, were an aerial for divine reception. And why shouldn't she think so, when all it took was a word of supplication from her for desire to coalesce and harden into fact? When Holmes had been sent packing, she asked to see him again, and shortly afterward he appeared at her window, waving and smiling, standing on air she assumed, though in truth on a window washer's platform he'd found vacant and irresistible. Also, against her parents' wishes, she was moved into LaBelle's room, and Holmes couldn't be kept from visiting family. A conspiracy of coincidence whispered around her, baffling her senses. She put in a request for her erstwhile friends, Greg and Ronny and Rob, to be infested with a pestilence of pinworms, then overheard Dr Nopper complaining to a nurse about a 'bunch of parasites'. Stinks? Possibly, though it only served to strengthen her belief in herself, her newfound religion. *Think* of what she could do with her connections, her direct line to Almighty beneficence. Matchmaking would be a snap. A girlfriend for Holmes, his long-lost mother, *whatever* he wanted. For Granny, she'd order up a new suit of skin, take forty years off and have it gift wrapped around her nice and tight. And how about sending Chamuel on a trip around the world, in a rowboat, with one oar? Never before had Rita felt such confidence and authority, wielding power raw and sweet, adult candy in *her* hands. Clearly, she had been favoured, chosen. No longer a Spanish Onion, a shadow's shadow, negative space, a mere girl. Look, tribute was piled around her. People she didn't even know had sent flowers, chocolates, toys, games. Liz Stronghill stopped by every day and brought her something new, an expensive dress or doll, and once, from the hospital gift shop, a fuzzy white finned thing called a 'Stuffed Soul'. Liz thought this was hilarious, and it was, and so was she. Rita hadn't known that laughter could be tossed so carelessly wide, star-gathering. Or that it could hurt so much. *Stop, Liz, ooh please, my sides.* Liz was so jokey and funny, slapdashing along.

'How would you like *me* for a mother?'

'Yeah! That'd be great, Liz. I'd love it.' No sooner uttered than Rita felt a sharp tug on that long tasselled cord inside her, guilt ringing in her head. *Thou shalt not betray thy parents.* At least that one wasn't written in stone. Though she knew her mother was jealous of Liz, coming up from the kitchen to check on her, and finding Liz *again* at her bedside, speaking low as Lilith in her daughter's ear. And later, bristling.

'What's *she* hanging around here for, eh? What's she want from you, that one? All this junk, give it back to her? Nothing's free, Rita, believe me. She thinks I can't buy you dresses? You hate dresses. Tell her to mind her own business. If you don't, *I will*.'

True. Rita did hate dresses. The ones her mother bought her, that were gaudy and fussy as lampshades, the word 'maudlin' spoken in fabric, and worse, spoken in Portuguese. Where did she find them, those dresses that were so foreign in style that when Rita wore one she felt she had a whole country layered on her back? A place she'd never even seen. But that was her mother. Not lacking in love. Her heartfelt labours on Rita's behalf made it ooze out of her like sweat, rank and offensive. And love had never been of much use in helping her see her daughter clearly. It waffled her vision, made her squint, caused her to lavish on Rita what she didn't need or want. Often her distracted, far-flung gaze overshot the girl standing directly before her. *Watch me*, Rita might say, performing some complicated acrobatic feat in their backyard apple tree, and Sofia *would* watch, full of pride, admiring her child's strength and ability. And freedom. But when Rita turned to collect from her an acknowledgement, a token of praise, the small coinage of attention, her mother's rapt look would have fallen away, down among the tree roots, given over to something else entirely.

Part of Liz Stronghill's bewitching charm was in her eyes. She had the focused intensity of a hypnotist, the obsessive awestruck gaze of a mother with a newborn. With it she fed Rita directly, a vixen-blue exhilarating substance. Though who was hooked? It was laughably obvious to Rita that Liz came daily as prayer to visit her because she had no choice. Rita had only to utter her name, the shortest command she knew, and Liz would appear. Rita's mother had it all wrong. As usual. The matter lay entirely in Rita's hands. It was all her doing.

Inches

IT WAS NEITHER bed head, high hair, nor the matitudinal optimism of the spine. What *was* it? Nothing short of a miracle. Short? Tsk, tsk. Growth, that most surreptitious of night-callers, had been putting on a show, cell clambering upon cell, hopping and bopping like fleas in flesh-coloured tights. The stage: Dinky Stink.

Pinch me, he breathed at his reflection in the mirror, because he had slept and dreamed tall for, um, so long. Tsk. He administered a swift round of slaps to the top of his head in the event of hallucination, brain sponge rising, fantasy frothing over, hope briefly and tantalizingly embodied, but nothing substantial. *Holy shit*, he whispered. His self-thrubbing had *not* caused him to bob back under the line of hockey tape stretched across the full-length (!) mirror that halved it into fact and fancy. The fact being his height. Yesterday. And the day before, and the day before that, his head submerged beneath a black untranscendable line revealing a creature from another world, truncated and clipped. But today ... *unfuckingbelievable!* The top half of his head had triumphantly crowned the surface and his reflected nose idled on the tape like a toe poised on a starting line, itching to take off. *Man*, this called for a celebration. Already in his head beer frothed over, spilling into his lap, *down* there somewhere; he could hear tires squealing, hubcaps bouncing like huge silver dollars into the ditch. He grabbed his jeans and yanked them on. Aaaah. The cuffs *man*, highwater, way north of his ankles. Jubilant Dinky howled and hurled himself into a spin, a pirouette that danced him out of the mirror's range, across the bedroom floor, faster and faster, a tornado that hit the window exploding it into a hard rain, flashing down.

Dolly was putting her teeth in, when she glanced out the bathroom porthole and saw Dinky scream past. At least he didn't have so far to go anymore to reach the ground.

Stone Hands

YOU GOOD AT SPORTS, Father? When you were a kid?

See these hands, Vic. Useless. Like boards. They repel ball-shaped objects. Other boys, nothing to it. *Throw, catch, throw, catch.* Automatic as heartbeats, as breath. Me, I'd choke every time. In the outfield, that glorious stretch of green, I'd yell, *It's mine, it's mine.* And I really believed that I could, just once, bring that sizzling soul-white missile home. It was never mine, Vic. All I ever caught was hell. Or ridicule.

You were meant for higher things, Father.

Higher than baseballs? I'll drink to that. *Saúde!*

Who's that now, in your lap?

This guy? St. Denis.

Where did you say you found him?

Outside. Stuck on the spire.

In the name of wonder. You mean somebody snuck into the church, whacked off his head, climbed the roof and stuck it on the spire? How bloody peculiar. What do you make of it?

Dunno. Kids. Some prank.

Very strange. Martyred twice, eh Denis, well here's to you. Vic'll have you fixed up in no time. I guess bodies are good for something. Take a drink in that condition and you'd have to piss out your neck.

You believe in miracles, Father?

Officially or unofficially?

Either way.

Nah.

Amber.

Goes down like silk.

This exact shade.

Bela.

A woman's hair, at a certain angle, how it catches the light.

Not Sofia's.

Undone, spilling over her shoulders, lovely.

Black, heavy, hangs down her back like a dead snake.
It is late last night the dog was speaking of you –
Aw Father, don't do that.

I'm not a whisky priest, Vic.

No, Father.

Someone left me this, on the back step. A foundling with a little black cap and a big dimpled belly. Quiet as a lamb. You don't suppose it's poisoned, do you?

Who'd want to do that?

Someone might. You know what I got in the collection last Sunday? Outside of the usual smatter of change, gum wrappers and fish hooks (once a condom)? A note, neatly folded, but written in a shaky scratchy hand that said, I *know* who you are. Good for them, I thought, that's more than I know.

This statue in our village fathered a child. It's true, Father, don't laugh. The mother, a young woman, very pious. She spent all her time in the church, praying and praying, prostrate before this one statue. Next thing you know, she's pregnant. Getting bigger and bigger. But it was a stone child, Father, with a stone heart. Like carrying a body of grief inside you. And the only way to get it out is through the eyes, the mouth. Tears and words. He came out in pieces.

You feel the warmth of His presence?

That'd be the booze, wouldn't it?

A divine medium.

You can change water into wine, right?

Cheap wine. Plonk. Wouldn't it be grand if I could produce a nice Bordeaux or a Chateauneuf du Pape?

I'm serious, Father.

I can change wine into blood, symbolically speaking. You know that.

Can you change one blood type into another blood type?

I give up. What are you really asking me, Vic?

What's your favourite female part?

Father!

Lips. Thin as lines, soft as pillows, I love a woman's mouth. Don't you?

Depends what comes out of it.

You ever notice that nun who sits in the front pew by the window, staring out, never hears a word I say?

The little one with the crooked habit?

She has a beautifully shaped mouth.

She's nuts, Father. They say she's the one who put itching powder in the hospital sheets, the flies in the raisin bread, the dirty pictures in Mother Superior's missal.

Ha! What's her name?

Sister Bernadette.

The little flower.

Wasn't that St. Theresa?

Whoever. You know, I've been thinking, Vic. Our saints here are a gloomy bunch. Too sombre. They could use a facelift. Maybe not as far as old Denis's face got lifted, but do you happen to have any wide, welcoming, heartwarming smiles in those paint pots of yours? I wouldn't mind being surrounded with lips like hers.

Father, you ever hear of something called the Lusty Man? You're Irish.

I think I heard his confession once. *Lord*.

How's Rita?

Changed. I tell you, you screw your brains out to get a kid, then before you know it, they turn right around and screw you back.

Vic?

Sorry, Father. Forgive me.

That's okay. Dash off a couple of Hail Marys, it'll clear the air.

When I was a boy attending mass, the host melting on my tongue like snow, I could actually *feel* it, this profound mystery entering my body, lifting me like a puppy by the scruff of my neck. My hands that were so useless, dumb as gloves, would suddenly feel awake, and full. Something so powerful coiling in and through my fingers. Something I thought was mine to keep.

Will you look at that. *Another* dead soldier.

The knuckleball.
The spinball, the curveball.
How about the knucklehead?
Like old Denis there?
So, Father?
Yeah, Vic.
Catch.

Just Like Romeo and Juliet

CURLED INTO A spaghetti clef, indicative of an inner music, the satisfying pitch of digestion, Eve slept. *Sans* eyelids, of course. What respectable snake would sport such an anatomical frivolity as an eyelid? Her pupils are concentrated into dark dots and her eyeballs are turned down. Actually, one is turned down and the other up, which gives her a comic and roguish air, though she is most definitely asleep. And utterly content, it would seem, a merry widow in her skin-tight gown, a middle-aged tummy bulge momentarily marring the normally svelte straight-as-a-gut figure. No matter. She'll work it off in a crescendo of dreams, a long undulate inner symphony.

When trembling, furry, four-footed dinner had arrived the night before, Eve and her mate Adam (who else? this is a tale of consummate monogamy) had eyed it with quiet yet keen snaky expectancy. But, hold on. Only one? Some bleeding heart rodent lover, responsible for the feeding, must have hidden the other quivering entrée in his pocket, smuggling it to the freedom of the schoolyard, mouse tartar on the lam. Fine, but what use is empathy unless well-rounded and all-embracing? Picture yourself in a similar situation, sitting with your date at a table in the Ocean House, waiting with mounting anticipation and appetite for your meal to be served, waiting and waiting, until finally *one single* order of toad-in-the-hole or spotted dick is slapped down in front of you. *Sorry, that's it.* What to do? You decide to share, to evenly dissect the toad or split the dick, and this is perhaps the social procedure, the anguinous etiquette, that these two serpentine diners were bent on, since Adam tucked into the tail end of the mouse, and Eve sank her jaws into its head. Many a time, Liz Stronghill and Blake Hardy had shared a single licorice twizzler. Starting one at each end they walked a candy bridge with their lips, nibbling their way to one another, quickly ravishing the distance between them and meeting in the middle with a triumphant and playful kiss. A pair of snakes striking out on a similar amatory, or simply gustatory gambit, would find themselves in trouble at about mid-mouse. Physiologically speaking, it's a one way street – teeth pointing like arrows in the direction of their stomachs – and the rule of this particular road is *eat or choke*. What's a girl supposed to do in a case like this, except to greet her lover as a sleeve greets an arm? Now you see him, now you don't. Oh Adam, Adam, wherefore art thou Adam? Oh woe! Oh lost love!

Oh well.

A door opened, breaking the sanctity of the classroom, the dim and eerie stillness that settles into a space usually roiled and churning with the unstoppable energy of children. No desks creaking, feet shuffling, pencils scraping, books slamming; no undercurrent of giggles and whispers and moans and suppressed shouts. Only a distilled and heady silence into which Roger Christopher stepped, his ensemble a little worse for wear after his night shift at the bar – a rip here, a splatter of creme de menthe there, an overall impression of wilt and drag. He rustled down the aisle and stopped before the terrarium to inspect the snakes. No. Make that snake. *Eve, you naughty thing*. He cocked an eyebrow and smiled down at her, in the dream she composes, a crescent moon suspended, his laugh a trill of night music in *terra incognita*.

To help them in their quest to find appropriate names for the class pets, Roger Christopher had suggested that the children consider famous literary or historical couples: Paris and Helen, Antony and Cleopatra, Dante and Beatrice, the Brownings, Lady Hamilton and Lord Nelson. *Who?* No one could accuse these kids of being overburdened with general knowledge, enisled here in paradise. Wayne and Shuster, someone lamely suggested, Roy and Dale? How about Gram and Ruthie, their own local perpetrators of unoriginal sin? Roger Christopher considers it interesting that the Lord got into such a lather about that snake Satan importing knowledge into Eden, as it must have been clear to Him even then that human beings are unteachable, obdurate as stones. At times, standing in front of this class, his own personal rock collection, he could feel himself fading away, losing substance, those impossibly hard heads eroding *him*. Death by ignorance, its crushing weight. Poor old Lucifer, the patron of teachers. He wonders what they will call Eve now that she's called her mate dinner. Long as a run-on sentence, Adam contained parenthetically in her middle, perhaps it was time to shift the focus to grammatical construction. The male of the species as subordinate clause. Knowledge, after all, *was* unavoidable, even in paradise. Even stone can take on language, be given a face (or two), a life of its own.

Picking a stray frequency out of the air, Roger Christopher began to hum. Then sing. The tag-end of some popular tune that caught in his head and unfurled like frayed ribbon out of his mouth, a single voice split into polyphony, coupling incestuously with itself, filling up the room with a progeny of sound.

Ruthie Stink abruptly turned off the truck radio, twisting the dial with a bone-breaking snap that choked some warbling sap in mid-refrain. Cloying, emotive music was the last thing she needed to hear. *Love!* Frankly, the subject sickened her – wasn't there anything else in the world to croak about?

She tore past the school, whirling by her own small self lodged in the past, a scowling child crouched alone, and unladylike, by the front door, white underpants showing. *I see England, I see France* ... I wish. Maybe the child was annoyed because Ruthie kept her there, a hostage holding her place in time like a bookmark. All Ruthie had to do was flip back a couple of chapters in her life and let the little girl dash inside to her classroom, where Mrs Rath – who had a face like one of Granny's burnt buns – was ordering the children to *move over, way over* in their seats to make room for their guardian angels. Picture a whole class unbalanced, perched off-centre, accommodating the unseen. Ruthie had felt so cramped, irritated because her envisioned angel was slovenly and overweight, a fatso who hogged all the space, his pressing thighs corralling her in her seat, making her want to scream. She remembers when the whole school formed a human rosary outside, each child representing a prayer which they had to recite when their turn came. Larry Lauder, who was a 'Glory Be', suddenly took off, streaking out across the road after a cat, and a car came flashing out of nowhere, and knocked him flying. Posted Larry directly to heaven, while they all stood watching, dumbfounded, every one of them useless as a prayer in a broken rosary.

This recollection had a chastening effect on Ruthie – she *was* a mother after all – and made her ease up on the gas pedal. She still managed to tear up the road, though, completely reorganizing the dirt and gravel, and where it was paved, she divvied it up along the broken line, both sides hers. She slid past the Ocean House, cruising the groove that countless carloads of teenagers had worn in the downtown circuit over an eternity of Friday nights. The main drag, so aptly named. On that same night of the week, any year, you could see Dolly and Burton Stink eating a bag of oranges and a six-pack of bananas while parked in this very truck in front of the Red & White. From this vantage-point they discussed, critiqued, and made various comments on the nasal topography of the passing citizenry. Here was one of those changeless, indeed ossified, rituals of small-town life against which you can mark your growth like nicks in a door frame. Ruthie remembers hopping out of Vincent's Five & Dime with a keyboard of candy cigarettes clamped between her lips, with a nit-comb Christmas present for her mother, with her very first tube of lipstick, violent red as a phial of blood, with a blush on her cheeks and a bag of black lingerie clutched in her hand – and there they'd be, Dolly and Burton, gawping out of the cab of the truck, mouths working like two fish in a bowl.

Pass me that banana there, Mother.

Which one?

That one.

This one?

Hell no, woman, the long one, *there*, with the spots.

There goes that Stronghill girl, still got it stuck in the air, hope it don't rain. Here.

Jee*zus*, the *long* one. You deaf as well as stupid?

Burton, get a load of that one.

Mmmmm, doggies, Mother. What a nozzle.

What a honker.

A trunk.

A prow.

A bloody peninsula.

The weight of it, you think she'd fall over.

I'm tellin' ya, she turns real quick, she'll slice that guy's ear off.

It's a purebred Wolinski, and that's a fact.

More engineering than a bridge.

Pass me that orange there, Father.

Which one?

It struck Ruthie with some force that a number of details which defined her life at present were extremely hard to credit. Details that bordered on the fantastic and required an almost promiscuously relaxed degree of sanity to take in. For one, that she was actually related to the above individuals, that she had married into the fish bowl, as it were, and now swam among them, the slimy and the scaly, an entire subhuman group with the personalities of sharks and the minds of anchovies. Why, oh *why* hadn't she marched right back into Vincent's and returned that bag of black underwear, eel-coloured, funereal, Stink bait? But surely this wasn't news. Hadn't she been present at her own wedding, and hadn't she noticed every Stink in the church mouth the words *I do* along with Gram, marrying her to a whole harem of aggravation? Apparently not. Blinded with romantic enthusiasm, not to mention gobs of Maybelline hailing into her eyes, she had walked directly, heedless of warning, into their vast chaotic embrace. Family as storm, as natural disaster. What was love anyway but a senseless enveloping flood that takes you for a rolling drunken tumble then leaves you beached and gasping for air, or dead as a plank? And here was another slivery detail, an assassin's dirk slyly inserted into her heart, another special delivery from the realm of the impossible. Could it be that her love for Gram had faltered? Was it conceivable that what she had considered to be boundless and endless, a love unlike any other, had rendered down into a homely imperfect object that she could examine coolly, callously? A small, insignificant, and expendable thing? Ever since she had grappled with that Innis George down on the checkerboard linoleum, her cheek pressed into the fossilized remains of a former Stink repast, she had begun to see her life differently. Possibly it was the unusual angle, the horizontal snake's eye view of the proceedings, that gave her a clearer vision, an unobstructed view of the unpleasant underside, the metaphorical snot stuck under the table. How unsatisfied she was, how restless! And with Gram raging above her, punching holes in the wall and threatening to smear Innis like paste on an open-face sandwich, his Stink physiognomy had never been so obvious to her before, the skull beneath the flesh a bone cradle exactly like the one out of which they all emerged looking basically the same. In a few years Gram would strongly resemble Burton, and then Grampa Stink, and eventually the monkey from which they all descended.

Yes, her eyes had been opened, but only to see the oddest of facts sperm-tailing into place, composing her life in hallucinogenic pointillism. Even to herself, Ruthie found it difficult to admit that she had developed an unforeseen yearning for Innis, a hunger as peculiar as the kind that makes some people devour bags of cement, or whole cars, piece by piece. Why *him?* Though she understood that desire

was incomprehensible, and once over the edge, deep as a dropoff. All
it took was the smallest step, the lightest shove, for what attracted
one person to another, what effected the most damage, was often a
blow so slight as to be invisible to others. A coy look tossed carelessly across a room, a flirty featherweight smirk that sends you reeling. Some lovers are driven wild by a mere curl, in hair or lip, by a
voice gravelly and rough, ground glass in the throat, by a dime of
flesh soft as a cupcake, by a Quasimodo slope of shoulder, an isosce-
les angle of elbow, by an uncanny resemblance to a former
girlfriend's chihuahua. You may simply never recover from the way a
certain woman flattens her vowels against you, or how a special man
rolls his r's right off his tongue and into your ear. So given the quirky
particularity of the playing field, why *not* Innis? Agreed, he was
hardly what you'd call a hunk – more a dab, a particle. Small, but
potent, potatoes. His charms were largely imaginary, though he
bore them with verve and dash, minting sexual currency out of the
nonexistent. He *could* carry a tune, if it wasn't too far, and he had
shown alacrity and fleetness of foot when his welcome in the Stink
household had worn thin as a G-string. Certainly he had qualities
that would attract a woman like Ruthie. All you needed was a body,
really. A nice bit of human upholstery in some eye-catching design,
and the 'stranger' motif was always popular with island women
shorebound overlong with the deadly familiar. Sheer otherness has
its allure. The unknown arriving like a bracing wind, a thrilling whispering breeze dropping out of the leaves and wrapping itself around
your neck. A crooning blue-eyed blustery guy in a seersucker suit
and white loafers. Then in a swift swirling turn revealing his intense
stormy side. Who *is* that man with the secrets sown into the coarse
twill of his dark and fertile being? A man of no fixed address, and
mysteriously employed, searching for an unspecified object.

Innis? Yeah. Why not?

It may not have been Ruthie's first intention to go searching for
Innis, trolling the backroads and streets in town with a single yearning note twanging in her head. When she booted the pigswill out of
the truck, that ankle-deep midden of orange and banana peels, bag-
fuls of time spent, countless Friday nights shucked and rotting on
the floor, all she knew was that she needed some air. Desperately
needed to get a fresh sweet reviving dose in her lungs, oxygen pure
and simple, unspoiled by a riot of Stink pungencies. On the farm, it

seemed, one's nose was always being rubbed in brutal malodorous facts, heaps of them generated by the decaying or defecating. What she needed was resuscitation from the universe at large, a place into which she could readily melt like a Venus spinning out of orbit. A woman alone in a fast-flying vehicle, what's to stop her from taking a lifelong detour? She could see herself skimming over the bridge, waving goodbye to the man in the control booth, maybe Holmes, the last Stink she'd ever have to lay her eyes on. But you can't leave your skin behind, your own marble-white skin would haunt you. Baby Stink, she'd never abandon him the way Emmy did Holmes, leaving a hole so big in his life that he's had to fill it with every piece of junk he could scrounge up. Why didn't she think to bring Baby along, his Stronghill skin scabbed with Stink overgrowth like parasitic lichen on a statue. Before taking off, she'd dropped him like an anchor in Dolly's arms, and that's what kept her within range, moored, unable to escape into an enticing distance except perhaps as it was embodied in another person. Such was her appetite, that when Ruthie found Innis, there's no telling *what* she'd do. She might eat him.

Why did the snake cross the road? Surely not because the frogs were greener on the other side. Nor because he wanted to end up flat as a belt, a one-dimensional character with a head like a buckle, cinching the revolting contents of some gourmet scavenger's stomach. Nor would he think the sinuous and winding road was itself a sacred place, worthy of a sacrificial pilgrimage. Oh, he wanted to get to the other side, all right, but why? Let's just say because his life was an epic in progress, a saga written lightly on stone, in dust, around the white nibs of grass, through the illuminated texts of fields, and he crossed the road like a serif crosses a 't'.

What Ruthie saw was an animate line, could have been a crack in the road come to life, a bolt of black lightning, that made her slam on the brakes and sent the truck spinning on loose gravel like a eager hoofer on dance wax. Ruthie provided the music, a long piercing aria spontaneously composed, a soundtrack for the brief preview of future events currently playing in her head: truck flipping off the road, truck hitting tree, exploding into flames, jump-cut to funeral, Stinks trashing funeral home and barfing in coffin, utter and final mortification, fade-out. It wasn't art. *But* it wasn't death, either.

Perhaps that childhood angelic presence was still with Ruthie, watching over her, holding her in place, a noumenal corpulence acting as the bumper pad that kept her safely on the road, for the only thing that died was the scream in her mouth when she realized the truck had stopped spinning. The only casualty had been the random garden growing on the dirt pile in the back of the truck, a weed-infested corn patch that spun out of the box like a gaily tossed toupee and landed smack in the centre of the road, a rogue island newly risen. Then, silence. Motes of dust drifting down. Heat rising out of the fields. Ruthie breathed in deeply, profoundly, filling herself to the toe nails and fingertips with a heady airborne infusion of light, grace, pollen, bug dirt. *Life.*

She stretched luxuriously, her own continued existence raying out gloriously from her hands, and reached for the ignition. Then her fingers stalled. What *was* that moving in the ditch, dark and unformed? Nah. Nothing. The wind teasing a bag, a ripped and bellying sail of plastic. But there was no wind. (Not yet.) Ruthie squinted hard, staring at the heaving black object as it rose up nameless into itself, withholding its identity until finally it burst into – a nun? *That* nun, Sister Whatsit, making a beeline for the truck before Ruthie could redeem herself from surprise and lock the doors.

For one who so lately had been travelling in loops and swirls, blazing her own complex and erratic trail, Sister St. Anne moved fairly fast and decisively to the truck, yanking open the door and hopping in, a May queen tagged with burrs and beggar's ticks, a daisy crown slung drunkenly around her wimpled head. She settled into the passenger's seat with the speechless familiarity of a gum-snapping sibling, her only gesture to reach out and switch on the radio. And there it was again, that *same* popular tune Ruthie had turned off earlier, the same sap warbling away, gnawing at the refrain like an old dog on a bone. Sister St. Anne began tapping her feet to the music, dipping her toes into the melody, began bobbing her head, bouncing her chin off the peppy lyrics. Then damned if she didn't start to sing. A tentative trickle of notes that soon flowed strong and deep. She turned to Ruthie, wide-eyed, amazed, as if she'd made some sort of discovery, had touched with her tongue something glittering at the bottom of the stream. She had a beautiful voice, was what struck Ruthie, ardent and full, invigorating, entreating all tributaries to join, and what the hell. When *was* the last time Ruthie had broadcast her heart and soul singing? She couldn't honestly remember. She used to sing all the time, happy to overflowing, one word embracing another, not this standing separately side by side, each hoarding its own little token of meaning. But song – *hey, hey, hey!* – Ruthie let her troubles and desires tumble away on the surge. She started up the truck and it began to sing, too, adding a bass ballast to their sistered voices, conjoined, full-throated, belting it out, volume cranked up and pouring out of the windows as they peeled off down the road, this unlikely medley braided into one.

Libation

RITA SQUEEZED THROUGH the large arched doors and entered the dim shadow-clotted church that was her second home. Familiarity brushed up against her, a dog-soft welcoming air. Quietly as one of the shadows, she moved to the font. Instead of dipping her fingers into the holy water and blessing herself in the usual way – that initial light touch of fingertips to the forehead like a gentle greeting from a stranger, an homage to and tapping of one's private thoughts – she put her face down into the bowl and laid her cheek on the water, touched her lips to it, stuck in her tongue like a root and began to drink. As brazen and blasphemous as this act might have seemed, Rita was only exercising rights that were hers, she felt, now that she had moved up, ascended in the incorporeal corporation. Power had been vested in her and with it came more sophisticated rituals, and liberties appropriate to her station. She would enter into the symbolisms of the church body *and* soul. How laughable, and trivial, her wanting so badly to join that boys' club. Greg had even approached her in the hospital, contrite, ashamed of the harm they had caused, to tell her she was *in*, no more conditions or initiations, she could consider herself an honorary boy. *Get lost*, she could scarcely be bothered answering, gazing down from a height, androgynous as an angel suspended in the stirred and beaten air of intense belief. Only months ago, only weeks, she had kneeled in this church praying and praying, asking the inert saints around her to send some slight sign, some indication that what she had been told to believe all her life was actually true. A twitch of a finger, a fluttering eyelid letting in a ray of light from the otherworld, this would have satisfied her. Confirmation would have to come from the saints since you couldn't get a straight answer from anyone else. *Uncle told me that religion is nothing but lies and fear. Is there really a God?* she asked her mother. Sofia answered carefully, *Many people believe so*. Her father, offended, closed his face against her. Chamuel simply shrugged, *Got me*. You'd think Chamuel would be proof enough, but he was a subject banned from family conversation, proof only to Sofia that what she feared might be true, that her daughter was mentally unstable, and to Victor that his brother must have interfered with Rita in some unspeakable and damaging way. Chamuel *was* an embarrassment, but Rita had been taught to entertain and give body to the idea of him. Sometimes she felt like a reliquary for other people's castoff fantasies, a storage space for all the stuff adults wanted to hang on to but didn't really find credible themselves.

And now she had this new information to check on, that if true would be a one-way ticket straight out of her family, and out of that cluttered oppressive house with its lumbering dead man driving her inescapably from one corner to the next. How she could be related to Liz Stronghill was beyond her, but only as far beyond as faith itself, only a short step away, albeit a dangerous one, over the edge. But imagine falling into the arms of such an adorable, besotted mother, sweet as Mary. Liz had been very persuasive staking her claim on Rita, and though they bore no resemblance at all to one another, Rita understood that she was the spitting image of her as yet unnamed father (that is, if his disparate parts were rearranged somewhat differently). What Rita needed, what would clinch it for her, was a divine nod of approval, something that would neatly snip those nagging ties of loyalty and dependence, and allow her to drift away, free. And she needed it immediately, Liz was waiting outside, engine revving, a map of the world spread open on her lap. So. She raised her head eagerly from her ceremonial refreshment to scan the church statuary. Who would it be? Which of her father's stone-faced gang would break down and, with a raised eyebrow or twitch of the nose, reveal to her the secret that Victor must have confided to them about her parentage?

It's true that Rita's eyes were rounded wide enough to catch the merest twitch of miraculous activity, but surely even a skeptic would have marvelled at what she saw. All round her a spiritual transfusion of the inanimate lit up faces as familiar to Rita as her own. On the saints, the Holy Family, the Sacred Heart, where before resided only a pale and mild reserve, a low-beam flicker of tranquillity and beatitude, there now shone an exultant happiness. The hallowed light of the church was absolutely wreathed in approval, everyone was smiling *at her*. And such smiles – gay and blossoming, glossy red lips so alive that words seemed ripe to burst from them, exhorting Rita to *Go. Run. Your mother is waiting. Don't stop. Don't look back. Don't* ... say no more, Rita turned and fled, and all that was left of her were a few drips of holy water that flew off her chin and splattered on the floor like star-shaped drops of blood.

I love the smell of gin, Liz thought, a dab behind the ears and a long one down the throat. The aroma is great, and mixed with a dash of Chanel, Martini #5, mmmn. Also, gin straightened out her tongue, which tended to flip words out every which way if she wasn't careful. But on a perfumed and wending stream of gin-breath they flowed out so nicely. An aura of gin around her head, frosty as the bottle it came in, and crisp, reminded Liz of her First Communion veil floating in front of her face like mist as she bounded down those very steps over there some twenty years ago. Her mother and father were part of the proudly smiling group gathered at the bottom of the stairs, parents snap-snapping pictures with their chunky box cameras. Liz remembers her mother's voice reaching up to her, 'Honey, slow down, *don't run.*' This was just before she took off, her slick and daintily bowed shoes launching her off the steps like a rocket. Laterally digressing, she disappeared out of everyone's viewfinder. In the family album you can trace, if not her flight path, then at least her silverheeled preamble on the runway. The first photo shows her heading the parade of children out of the church, beaming like a child bride with a bouquet of beads binding her reverently clasped hands. In the next, she's broken away from the pack, feet dancing down the stairs, hands now flung open, rosary yawning wide as a lasso. Then, a blur, a white froth, heels only pinched with feathery spurs of light, flutterkicking out of the frame. The other children following behind, heads cocked at the same angle, wearing identical expressions, appear interested but unsurprised to see Liz fly off. Freshly initiated into the rites and mysteries of the church, perhaps anything seems possible, and to them this may only be one of many wonders to come. Stilled here in a communion of polite credulity, little do they realize that they are perched on the very brink of the ordinary and uneventful. As for Liz, she broke an arm, chipped a tooth, banged up her knees, got dirt on her dress, lost the tiny metal Jesus off her rosary, and was left with an overall impression of religious commitment as being an insufficient container for the plenitude of her enthusiasm.

Liz indulged in another dab of gin, scenting the interior of her throat, and tipped the bottle to drop a fragrant splash down the front of her dress for good luck. She glanced up at the still-empty steps, foot tapping anxiously on the accelerator. What if Rita's father caught her sneaking in and questioned her? What if he was suspicious and made her stay, locked her in a broom closet? Rita hadn't explained why she wanted to visit the church before they left town, but as Liz was determined to be a perfect parent – a paragon of reason and understanding, no gratuitous yelling, and of course an unfailing provider of fabulous desserts – she felt it was her duty to support the child's spiritual needs. That is, as long as she didn't want to join the Doukhobors or something. No daughter of hers was going to fling off her clothes and march around in public. Liz would definitely draw the line through that one – no Doukhobors allowed in *her* car.

Ahem, was that *her* car? Why yes, gin was metaphor in a bottle, it dissolved barriers and promoted the miracle of connection. Apply liberally to stubbornly discrete spots and soon they'll sprout hyphen-thin arms to gather in the dissimilar. I am you, you are me, your troubles are my troubles, your Triumph TR4 is *my* Triumph TR4. That at least is the philosophy of gin unstintingly splashed around. Right, Liz thought, let's have none of this greedy *yours* and *mine* business, as she hopped into Innis' car so conveniently parked at the hospital, key in the ignition, when she had Rita discharged. Besides, blue was her favourite colour. Blue roses, blue popsicles (weeping inky pools in the glove compartment where she'd tossed them, the first of those fabulous desserts), and the great *blue* yonder, the destination for which she and Rita were headed in this rattling, clunking, one-eyed blue beast.

Travel. Liz had dreamed for years of getting off this island, years she's worked in that crummy restaurant, saving for this day. She was sick to death of the claustrophobia, the shrunken expectations, of being known so thoroughly that it seemed every cell and corpuscle in her body was accounted for, all grist for the rumour mill, raw material for pure fantasy. Your life wasn't even your own here; it was a communal source of entertainment. Liz took another swig. To hell with connection. I am *not* you. You are *not* me. Bug off. (She'd hang onto the Triumph, though.) Liz glanced down and the whole world was spread out on her lap. No matter that it was a historical map pinched from Rita's classroom, detailing the routes of famous explorers, Columbus, Champlain, Marquette and Joliette. Next billing, Liz and Rita Stronghill. Mind you, it wasn't fame that Liz was after, but rather those enticing uncharted spaces into which she and Rita would disappear like two ghosts. Some people want to lose themselves, and on such a map there were whole continents of anonymity in which to do it.

Liz was itching to honk the horn, praying instead, a kind of spiritual honking, for Rita to appear. Please, come on. By Jesus, *now*. They had one more quick sidetrip to make before they could leave, a stopover at the graveyard. Liz wanted Rita to meet her real father, to pay her respects. Though she hadn't meant to give her the impression that Blake was still alive. *Is. Was.* Damn those tenses. Such paltry insignificant words to contain the whole of the past and the rich unfolding present. A slip of the lip and *naturally* one might pop out instead of another, reviving a dead man with a peck, a tap, a one-word spell. Well, Rita would understand. *She* was a perfect daughter.

And there she *was*, bursting through the church doors, running down the steps. But wait, those stairs. Liz had to warn her. What should she say? How do you keep a child from inevitable harm, from disaster you can see coming as clearly as a stranger with malevolent intent? How do you stop her from spilling out her precious life in front of you, down the length of the stairs, when all you have is gin-soaked lovesick language, a useless net to catch her in? Why, you have to resort to that good old parental mantra, you have to make your words hard as bullets and absolutely riddle her with them. You have to shout *don't don't don't* and stop her dead in her tracks.

Weather

CONJURING, Roger Christopher raises his hands and floats them like clouds over the open pages of a book. He feels the heat rising, a stir of warm air through the lace of letters, a slight breeze coursing down the spaces between the lines.

Out at the graveyard, Gladdin Doan touches his son's headstone, running his fingers over the engraved name, the dates, eyes closed, reading blind. The heat of the day rushes up into the stone like the remembered life of his boy, Perlen, suffusing it in greeting.

Father Finn and Victor Cabal, momentary conspirators in a drunken whim, make-up artists with their brushes and pots of red paint scattered around them, are sleeping it off in the vestry, while outside a branch rubs against the window, writing an invisible and urgent message.

A magnum of sunlight spills through the window of the cruising Stink truck and paints the throats and chests of Ruthie and Sister St. Anne gold as birds.

Holmes Stink, seated crosslegged on the salvaged hardwood floor of the *Marylou* – memory of water plumping the grain – and polishing a brass hand lamp, looks up from his work, sniffing the air. A subtle telltale creaking of the boat, a scribble of wind here and there slanting ominously, a pessimistic hand diving into the channel – you didn't have to be a seer to read what was coming.

Weather. In one of its more histrionic moods. It arrives like the witch *not* invited to the christening, feathers ruffled, hair askew, mad-eyed, mascara running rivers, a long zephyrous garment trailing. What *has* it been missing, *what* on earth is everyone looking for? Brooding, plotting, it picks at the lake, slaps a few boats against the dock, yanks open a window and peers with a bright gleam into the depths of a room, turns over all the leaves on a tree to read their silver palms. It finds a coffin-shaped box of papers behind the town garage and paws through them, hurling them up into the air, scattering them wildly in every direction. (Everyone's an amateur archaeologist, a snoop.) *What's* the big deal, it thunders, *what's* all the fuss?

It settles on its haunches, glowering, hazy-headed, heated with exasperation, excluded. *Nice day*, someone comments carelessly, passing through, and is quietly marked for a lightning bolt through the head. *Nice!* The weather does not want to be *nice*. It wants to slit open the secret of this day from tip to stern and spill its umbles. It wants to leap onto centre stage – *Ta da!* – and be the thing that is missing, the buried treasure, the lost and the dead resurrected. It wants to be, as they say here in their vulgar tongue, *some kinda weather!*

Just wait. It slides into the shadows, cooling its immense heels. Just you wait.

Floating Heads

Yak yak yak.

Words begetting words begetting more words. One thing, the guy didn't need a body, just a head, a convenient place to keep his mouth. He'll drown this time for sure, thought Holmes, because he can't shut up. He probably wouldn't know what to do with a body anyway. Holmes hadn't witnessed a dogpaddle technique like his since Gram chucked Duke Stink overboard during a fishing trip because Duke was drooling on his socks, which is where Gram keeps his snack, two blackballs and a red hot in bas-relief slung around his ankle. Avarice, thought Holmes, gluttony, greed, ambition ... volubility? Surely that was one of the deadly sins, too. Lethal. Holmes pictured himself blue-faced, tongue sticking out, strangled by a stocking-thin, tediously long run-on sentence. *What* was the guy trying to say? He wished he'd just *spit it out*.

There are two kinds of people in the world, Innis decided as he dogpaddled circles around Holmes, who was treading water so effortlessly his head seemed merely to rest on the surface like a head sitting on a glass plate. Two kinds of people – talkers and listeners. Of the former, there were rare individuals, such as himself, who could serve up, without notice, a veritable feast for the ears, gourmet discourse several courses long, complete with *bon* bon mots and salty pungent sallies. Holmes had ears like bowls waiting to be filled, and, sighing with resignation, Innis complied.

What a blockhead, he thought.
What a motormouth, he thought.

Days it had taken Innis to corner Holmes, who had finally agreed to meet with him, but in his cornerless office with the fluid furniture, about twenty yards from the dock. Okay, Innis was game, his make-believe muscles buoying him up like water wings. To break the ice, and thank God it *wasn't* winter, and to give Holmes some idea of his intellectual range, he began with some small talk. Very small. Bite-size excerpts from an endless and minutely detailed history of the canapé. Was it in 1942, when mushroom caps got stuffed, that he lost Holmes? Or was it 1954, the year zucchini boats were launched in the *New York Times*? All Holmes knew was that one moment Innis was going on and on about *cochons en chemis* and angels-on-horseback, and the next he was talking about standing stones and a chalk giant in Dorset with a thirty-foot phallus. Man, he hated swaggering, inflated, masculine banter. Male bonding? No thanks. Elmer's glue-all was much more useful.

Decapitated by the waterline, staring at each other as if through a fog, trying to discern some mirrored and recognizable feature. Blood brothers? Water brothers? They'd have to cut deeper than this.

'Yeah?' said Holmes.

Circling, circling, orbiting around Holmes, the still centre – *how* did he do that? (Easy, when you're standing on a reef of tar barrels.) He was panting out facts and shreds of information more raggedly – it *was* an effort – but yet felt himself closing in, warming to his theory. Not *his* theory exactly, Inch had done all the legwork, but it was Innis who would locate the actual 'x' on the map. And, with the help of this deep-delving Stink, it was *he* who would find something amazing, something of a kind never before found in this country, engraving that x on it like a resuscitating kiss planted firmly on stone lips.

Innis opened his mouth again to speak and a fistful of water pounded in, a helping of surf that filled his face and surprised his throat, his laryngeal reflex sending it directly, unchewed and unheralded, to his stomach. He gasped, choked, inhaled another wedge of the lake, and promptly sank out of sight.

Le this and *la* that. Sexing words was weird enough, Holmes thought, but churches? Churches decorated with genitalia, copulating couples, bestiality … weren't soffits and fascia enough?

Holmes was keeping a watchful eye on his recuperating guest, in case a stray drop of water should fly up his nose and finish him off for good. He figured it wouldn't take much and Innis seemed bent on drowning himself. Alarming, this habit he had of tossing his life away in front of Holmes, discarding it like an old rag for him to pick up, saviour as domestic. Nor had he stopped talking, nattering even as Holmes dragged him to the *Marylou*, chuntering and gnawing away in an effort to sharpen whatever point it was he was trying to make.

Treasure hunter, they thought simultaneously, and none too kindly.

The brass hand lamp was charming, a brightly polished cup with a window in it. It charmed Holmes, at any rate. He ran his finger over the small curved handle at the back, felt a ghostly knuckle lodged there, belonging to the hand of the sailor who once clutched the lamp walking through the ship's hold at night, whistling quietly to himself (much as Holmes was doing), his head a tumblerful of dreams. Holmes held the lamp up and put his eye to the window. Inside, he saw a dancing path, pins of light, children coming home from school late of a winter afternoon, tin lanterns swaying like censers dispelling the gloom. Further back, behind them, he saw link-boys bearing torches down labyrinthine streets, mullein stalks greased and lit, cursing away the terrible ancient dark with snapping flaring tongues. He saw children, as far back as he had the power to imagine, lighting the way. But he didn't see Rita.

Where was she? Why this sense of something gone wrong, the air so heavy, a dead body pressing against him? Worry scored a staff of lines across his forehead with its harrowing claw.

'Well, what do you think?'

'About what?'

Innis sighed, staccato, his teeth were still chattering. He might have cornered Holmes physically, but getting a grip on the guy's attention was like trying to hold smoke. 'About me going down with you, I've got a pretty good idea where it might be.'

'It?'

'What I've been *telling* you about. The two-headed stone man, the missing Mr x, Mr Iron Age Artifact.'

'I thought you might want to find your, um ...'

'My phallus? Yeah, I'd love to get my hands on that again. For personal reasons, you understand. Yeah, let's look for that, too.'

'You won't find it.'

'Why not? The current, you mean? Needle in a haystack?'

A pin prick. *He* said it.

'I suppose you're right. How appropriate though, eh? I mean, the male principle uniting with the female, the great womb of the sea.'

Principals might carry on like that where he comes from, but, 'This is a lake.'

'Same idea.'

'Not if you're drowning.'

'What do you mean?'

'Takes longer to drown in seawater than lake water.'

'Come on.'

'Different chemical process.'

Wait, this is a Stink speaking, he doesn't know this.

'I knew a fellow from Homer who drowned sitting on his front porch, feet up on the railing, watching his field of corn grow.'

'*Sure.*'

'It can happen, delayed complications, you might want to take note. Hours, even days later, the blood quietly diluting, the heart beating slower and slower, until finally it stops.'

Innis stared at Holmes, a wisp of fog lifting, some of his own intelligence reflected in the man's face.

'So, whereabouts is this great find of yours?'

'Near here, I think. I've already checked on a few possible places, this is the last. If you give me a piece of paper, I'll draw a map to show you.'

'I already have a map.' Holmes reached down, slipped a wad of paper out from under the chair leg, and handed it to Innis.

'Very nice, heh, but a generic map isn't ... hey wait, this is it! Where did you get this? Who else knows about it?'

Holmes shrugged. When Stink lips clamped down on a subject, there was no point in trying to pry even a syllable loose.

'All right, we better go then. Before somebody else beats us to it.'

'Can't in this weather.'

'What? It's gorgeous out. Absolutely beautiful.' A finger of wind twirled his hair playfully. 'We'll only go down for ten, fifteen minutes, just to scout around, then head straight back in.'

'*I'll* go down, you stay in the boat.'

'Okay, okay, but remember, it's *my* discovery. Don't worry, you'll be well paid. You know, this will make my name.'

'I suppose you want to be out standing in your field?' Ha! Now there was a hoary old Stink joke. Sometimes Stink conversations were nothing more than punchlines cobbled together, the body of the jests long since forgotten, a family code that provoked instant amusement. He and Gram were particularly good at it, wisecracking lines back and forth, giggling uncontrollably, almost a foreign language to an outsider.

'Yes,' said Innis, '*Yes*, I do.' He didn't get it.

'Poof,' Holmes said, snapping his fingers, 'you're a pile of shit.'

A long thrilling glissando into silence. Though not silence exactly – rather, another world of sound. More intimate, immediate, the *boom boom* of your heart pounding in your head. Fish clicking and grunting and grinding their teeth, not the mute citizens of the water that they might appear to be from above. The waterline is the boundary, but sound is not coterminous; immediately it is other, ghostly, travelling to the ear faster, apparently sourceless. You can't rely on it to guide you, following crumbs of noise that expand, exploding direction. Easy underwater to lose your way, and your self.

Holmes knew well enough how disorienting a wreck could be if it was lying upside down. Somehow you didn't expect that, an invitation into a tumbled world, confusion, panic, but not all boats settled neatly and conveniently upright on the bottom. More likely resting in pieces than peace, broken open and dismembered over a distance and at varying depths. And some, if intact, were best avoided altogether. Especially a sidewheeler with its maze of dark cabins and saloons, a fascinating and deadly funhouse from which you might never emerge.

Holmes descended thirty feet, forty feet, deeper into the philosophical element. Now who said that? Not Holmes, he didn't equate this kind of profundity with thought. Let the carp do the thinking. He was content to maintain a meditative alertness. Comfortable, familiar, but like a medieval man submerged in an atmosphere animated by spirits, good or ill, he kept careful watch. It wouldn't do to get fouled up in a ship's rigging, to run out of air, to burst an eardrum or a lung, to get the bends, the chokes, or the narks. Nitrogen narcosis. Pleasant at first, exhilarating, but before you can say rapture of the deep – *hey presto!* – you're Poseidon gallantly offering your mouthpiece to some dark curvaceous deadhead.

Once, a garden of arms. That, at least, hadn't been a hallucination, for Holmes had seen them clearly and clear-headed extending surreal as stalks with open hands out of the silt toward him, a bed of impaling embrace. Startled, he had ascended too quickly and earned his first case of decompression sickness. The whole length of that night he spent curled foetal in the hold of the *Marylou*, pressure bruises blossoming the clenched curve of his body.

But *arms*, what a strange cargo. Maybe somebody else's punchline embedded in history, the sick joke being an ever present stowaway in the human mind. *Quick, all is lost, send arms.* Holmes had heard of a place that makes heads for memorial soldiers, who apparently lose them with some frequency, so why not, perhaps some limbless Shiva of the north was yet awaiting completion. That was it, though, the seductive draw of the deep, never knowing when you go down *what* you'll find. And as for something particularly sought after, well, good luck. Things were rarely where you expected or imagined them to be. That 'x' so confidently anchored on the map, what would Holmes see when he slipped through it, transparent as an illusion? Anything at all? Difficult to catch on a map a place in motion. Down here, even a two-headed stone man can become a travelling man, an emigrant of the lake bottom, a roving Celt from the old world missing these many years from his Janus-faced family. Let's say he went to sea as ballast, travelling nth class like so many of his countrymen, and like so many of them was lost, tumbling into this wayward afterlife. A fugitive. If Holmes found him, would he want to turn him in? See him imprisoned in a museum or private collection, Innis rounding out the sin and definition of vainglory with his every inflated word? Holmes didn't see much point in that, really. Didn't see how this inscrutable figure could be made to bolster crackpot theories (and reputations) about old religions and lost knowledge. (Aha, Holmes had been listening, after all.) The idol's lips may be parted as if to speak, but they're still made of stone, the secrets of his vanished world petrified on them. Admit it, evocative is usually all you get. Holmes realized that. How often had he tried to draw warmth and connection out of odd bits of flotsam, offering at least a gesture of remembrance? But these things we make and hoard and covet, they're poor vessels. Human life spills out of them prodigiously, like blood under water so black you don't even recognize it for what it is. Death. Its pendant flowing.

Clearly this stone man was a survivor, his brain pan a chalice that held the current libation, whether sacrificial or lakewater. Whatever, he didn't care. He made his way, stirred his inanimate stumps somehow. But Rita! Perishable skin, precious breakable bones, *that's* who needed to be found. What was he doing down here anyway, encased in rubber, enveloped in his own breath, as self-absorbed as Innis was in his element? Escaping the blather above? All the blather, the prattle, the demands, the confusion, that crowded into and clawed at the air, and not simply Innis's considerable contribution. But maybe he was just another trespasser down here, another despoiler, and not a dual citizen as he had thought.

If he wanted an answer to his questions, at least to the obvious, the dark shape of a sunken schooner loomed before him. *Of course*, here was a ship he'd never entered before, a virgin wreck, as they're called. The x of the map lay like invisible drapery over one window, an enticing passage for a mystery-driven man to slip through. (A frogman would a-wooing go. Uh-huh.)

Holmes touched her bow lightly, traced the brass nameplate with his watersoft fingers, flesh filling in the interstices the letters made in making the name. Then he gave a decisive push and a brisk backward kick of his finned feet as he turned away, and up. *Up.*

Innis had assessed the hand lamp (not worth much), as well as the other antiquities on board, including the perishable ones in the fridge – yuck! He had, snickering like Oilcan Harry, turned the tiny golden key that unlocked Holmes' five-year diary, expecting to find a wealth of dirty secrets pertaining to his personal and propertied life, only to discover, in Holmes' childish hand, the weather. Days and days of weather, described in almost psychoanalytic detail, the idiosyncrasies of a disturbed personality. *Anthropomorphism*, Innis snorted, *how primitive*, and he tossed the diary overboard. Then he had perused a shelf of diving books, flipping quickly through the pages, and now hopped about on deck in full regalia – farmer johns, chicken vest, cold water hood, three-fingered mitts, tanks, a weight belt, a depth gauge, a compass, and a knife, which he was using to stab and slash at the air, extricating himself from some envisioned entanglement. If only Ruthie Stink could see him now. How manly he was, a Lloyd Bridges decked out in his business suit of the deep, cut for adventure, sculpting his fine form. Emphasis on fine, as in bone, for the wet-suit belonged to Holmes and didn't cling with all that much fidelity to Innis. It sagged in places that only a robust and sympathetic imagination could provide compensation for.

Innis looked over the side of the *Marylou* at the water, which lay deceptively flat and clear. 'Pellucid,' he announced to a passing gull. Here was a small gem of a word he'd always wanted to display, but couldn't seem to find the right setting for it. The one time he tried it out on a girlfriend's complexion, she misheard him. Putrid, she asked? *Putrid* skin? And after that her skin was not only pellucid, but transparent, as he never saw her again. Of the lake, Innis should have spoken with greater exactitude, with greater care. He might have said treacherous, perilous, unsound – life-preserving adjectives cautioning restraint, tolling warnings. But no, clambering up on the bow of the *Marylou*, he would insist on *pellucid*. He would leap in, directly through the skin of the word, shattering its meaning. Immediately, his mask fogged up and stuck to his face like a plunger. His ill-fitting wet-suit flooded with water and wax buildup in his ears made his ear drums bulge like cervical caps – painfully. While his weight belt performed its simple duty of taking him straight to the bottom, his instant recall of those diving books provided entertainment for the trip. Again, he was flipping quickly through them, seeing a diver in serious trouble and exhibiting 'non-problem-solving behaviour', in other words drowning like a fool, his face frozen into a mask of utter and complete disbelief.

The wind wasn't the only one sighing. Corporal Leonard Watts, planet Earth, summer of his discontent, sighed in unison, and then burped discreetly, one plump finger straddling his lip like a muffler. '*Ex-cuuse me*,' he said to the same passing gull that Innis had tried to impress. Leonard was glad of the gull, for he had in similar gastric distress excused himself to lamps and filing cabinets. One wanted to address the living, after all. Though solitude was still no excuse to let the civilities slide, the decencies and rules of conduct, the whole delicate webbing that kept our mutual regard taut. The temptation *was* great, but Leonard had absolutely *no* intention of sitting out here in the middle of the lake picking forbidden fruit out of his nose. He had the self-control, the resolve to resist such temptation, for he was a man of the law. Other people? *Very* disappointing. They hurt each other. They stole, the lied, they broke things, they had *no* manners. Why, only last night someone, as if to underline the obvious, had knocked the head off the unknown soldier in the bandshell park. What kind of depraved individual would commit such a heinous and disrespectful crime? And this morning, Dot Spry saw the head staring in at her, propped on the ledge outside her window, and nearly had a heart attack. Leonard shook his own neatly coiffed and precisely hatted head sadly, and a little too abruptly. He had a delicate constitution and this motion provoked in him a case of the hiccups. 'Darn,' he said. *Hic.*

He certainly didn't relish his duty today, though he enjoyed being out in the police boat, *hic,* gently rocking – my, how the wind had picked up – and he wondered if a tad of fishing might not be in order while he waited. Really though, *hic,* he found it incredible that Holmes Stink, of all people, would kidnap a child and do, gosh, who knows what to her, and that he, *hic,* Leonard Watts – old 'Farty' Watts, as he was called at the station – had the most unpleasant duty of arresting him. *Hic.* He liked Holmes, Holmes was nice, what if he hurt his feelings? But then, he had to think of the parents, too. Foreigners, but still, they were out of their minds with worry. Leonard sighed again. Hiccuped again. He shifted slightly in his seat and reached for his wallet, which is where he kept THE PAPER BAG. Other men might carry condoms in their wallets, but Leonard found a paper bag much more useful. In fact, no other cure worked for him, *and believe you me,* he'd tried them all. Humming show tunes while holding his nose, holding his breath and thinking of baseball, holding his gun to his head, terrifying himself with mildly existential thoughts. Nothing worked. But this. He unfolded THE BAG gingerly, fastidiously, and placed it over the top of his head.

Hic, Leonard said from within. Pause. '*Ex-cuuse me.*'

Venus giving birth to twins? A two-headed figure, at any rate, rose out of the waves, one head alert and crying out, while the other slumped forward, blue lips betraying a difficult passage. The water was choppy, the waves playful, as if eager to catch and sink the words that the livelier head was attempting to toss over them. Words that were heavy with alarm, desperate, not much fun.

A police boat. Holmes couldn't believe his luck, though he

doubted that Innis himself had any left. Poor fool. What had ever possessed him? Clasped in his arms, so close, and yet he was an even greater mystery to Holmes than the spurned idol.

'Leonard!' Holmes shouted, sending his voice sailing into the testy wind and over the tagging slapping water. Holmes would recognize THE BAG anywhere, and of course the gentleman it contained, the unknown policeman.

'Leonard, *help*.' Oh yeah, '*please*.'

Index of Instances

ROYALTY RAN LIKE liquid gold under most people's noses and they didn't even notice. On the Stink farm alone, one might meet a Duchess and a Duke, two Ladies, a Prince, and, a little fanfare here, a *King*. And not just any Heinz 57 sovereign, either, not one of those lie-in-the-shade-and-gnaw-his-haunches kind of ruler, but a king who had made a name for himself – Richard 11, a.k.a. Dick the Dog. Now Dick was a mover and shaker (when wet), blessed with a befitting regal air, an enterprising spirit, excellent connections, and a residence in town as well as the country. Well-born, he was a creature of pedigree, his genealogical roots established in the fertile soil of a mythologically enriched past. His great-grandfather had been an Irish mist-swilling pooka, who had arrived in the diaspora, part embellishment, part wolfhound (altogether a dog of parts). This might account for Dick's spotted coat, an archipelago of lost islands floating in a sea of fur, a map of an imaginary land. Although pinstripes, if that were possible on a dog, might have suited him better. He had a nose for business (and self-promotion, what other dog has a dessert named in his honour?), an entrepreneurial instinct, and, not incidentally, he carried a briefcase. Dick would no sooner be caught with a bone in his mouth than he would, if human, be caught with an old chestnut. And what, pray tell, did he carry in this briefcase? Basically, it was a dossier of edible materials, among them some research papers, of which there seemed to be a great many floating about lately, as well as a few top-secret and sensitive, literally quivering, items. He had no need of business cards as he distributed his royal signature liberally, x marks the spot, warm and steaming on a pole or tree. King John couldn't have done any better.

Gaze past your thighs, your kneecaps, into the sub-country in which you wade daily, striding unconsciously through swirling political currents, subtle treacheries and insurrections, and you'd be gazing into Dick's realm. You might be surprised at the level of activity. Dick wasn't. He was vigilant, keeping an eye on the lower orders, on the sly manoeuvres and scuttling stealth of the insect, rodent, and feline populace. Nor was the lumpenproletariat of human limbs discounted, especially the feet that delivered only kicks, the hands that paid tribute in pats and snacks. Dick knew the dirt, all right, the base rumours, the smell and lay of the land directly south of the sole. Ranging through town on any given day, on *this day*, he gathered intelligence at random. Arranged for future reference, his impressions might appear thus:

Bitch. And he wasn't talking about that wiener dog he'd had over on Baxter, cute as a schnitzel, dinner and date rolled into one. No, he meant that bitch, Ruthie, blasting through town in the truck. She nearly flattened him, turned him into a road rug, brought his highness most low. On purpose. And singing her lungs out, *good Dog*, he'd heard crows in better voice than her. Dick had to wonder what Gram saw in that woman, she obviously didn't see much in him anymore. Gram was no easy read, either, Stinks are deceptive. She was skipping the hard bits, the metaphysical patches. Gram was like *War and Peace*, only shorter. Women! What *did* they want? Whatever it was, he had his doubts about that nun helping her to find it. She couldn't even find her own soul. Though *she* did have a lovely voice, made him want to howl right along. And that time outside the hospital chapel when she fed him a handful of hosts, chanting, *This is my body, this is my blood.* They were delightful, like nibbling on butterflies, like having tea with Queenie. Though personally Dick would have preferred a steak, rare, hot off the barbecue. Spiritual food is so overrated. There are bodies, and then *there are bodies*.

Cabal. Small calves missing, and parents baying like sick hounds. A Stink kid, no great loss. But Rita, tsk, a heartbreaker. She was the one who gave him his first taste of gorgonzola and garlic, transforming his foul doggy mouth into a poet's garden. Such is the breath of kings.

Christopher, Roger. That cur. He makes Dick's hair stand on end, gives him the creeping Fifis. Leaves no scent, smells of nothing. Dick found his dress in the confessional when he trotted in for his weekly session with Father Finn. Dick, the confessor, donning the dog collar – *woof, woof!* Sin was safe with him, *hey, fire away*, his ears were long, he'd heard everything. No surprise, really, to find that the priest was actually an Anglican ('I couldn't resist'), that he hadn't meant to carry the ruse this far, that he might have to skip town soon, that he was thinking of becoming a surgeon next. ('*Snick-snack*, I think I've got the makings.') He wouldn't lie to a dog, would he? *Bless me, Dick, for I am sin*. Roger Christopher. Not a word the so-called teacher utters that isn't split, equivocal. *Bolingbroke says, sit. Bolingbroke says, roll over. Play dead.* Creep. Dick tried to work the dress into his briefcase, but it wouldn't fit. So he sank his teeth into the bodice and dragged it down to the lake. Then, adieu. Farewell. Sweet …

Prince. The dauphin of dogs. His pup, his whelp … ah, but children are such heartaches. They suck the marrow right out of your bones. And the more they grow, the greater the disappointment. Did Prince actually *snap* at his noble father the other day, at *us*, king of the mutts. That boy was getting too big for his dewflaps. Of course, it was the disreputable company he was keeping. That mongrel, Baby Stink. What a lowlife. Why, he didn't even have a name. (He had *rank*, mind you, in abundance. Too bad Ruthie didn't stay home once in a while and change a diaper.) Nothing for it, Dick would just have to nip it in the bud before it flowered into one of those boy-dog relationships. And he knew exactly which bud to nip.

Stink, Holmes. Speaking of bad smells, how Holmes came to be in the custody of Farty Watts was surely a ripe conundrum. Holmes a criminal? Come, come. Here was the one human a dog could safely shake paws with without that feeling of imminent betrayal, a trip to the vet's, or, more likely, to the bottom of the lake. Dick hadn't forgotten how Holmes had once given him a whacking great bone he'd found. The missing link, and Dick ate it. Talk about vintage, late Cretaceous, an excellent millennium. The ancient earthy bouquet haunted his nose still – heady stuff, time itself dissolving in his mouth. *Hang on, old pal,* Dick set down his briefcase outside the jailhouse window and smiled in at Holmes like a lawyer with a finely honed argument in his teeth, *this won't take long.*

Weather. By Dad, Dick hated it when the prowling troublemaking wind raked its fingers the wrong way up his back.

Wenches. Snooping along the shoreline, following his own nose around this spit of land here with a *hey nonny no* and a … *oho!* What's this, a naiad convention? *Wuzah wuzah.* The scenery! If he were a wolf, he'd whistle. If he were Duke Stink, that old whorehound, he'd hie himself down there and hump a few legs. So this is where they've all gotten to, disporting themselves in the lake, and not a stitch on. Very fishy. The better half of the Stink truck was married to that tree over there, and a sports car was bobbing in the water like a blue buoy. Dick supposed this qualified him as a prime witness. He positioned himself to indulge in some keen observation, and panting, barometer rising, straight up. *Such* babes, truly, he was smitten. His tongue lolled out of his mouth like a lover's red hot proclamation.

Worthington St. Former residence of Fluffy Wolinski. Heh heh.

LaBelle Stink Sans Merci

'What *are* loins, anyway?'

'What?'

'I mean, *where* are they?'

'Red & White, forty cents a pound.'

'*On* a man. You know, as in, he girded his mighty loins.'

'I dunno. Down there somewhere, I guess. Why?'

'I was reading this book in the Ocean House, a romance, supposed to be about women in love, but all the guy kept talking about was loins, loins –'

'Ruthie, I'm shocked. *You* were reading a book?'

'Get lost.'

'That's exactly what I was trying to do before you ran me off the road.'

'Lookit, Liz, I didn't run *you* off the road. You were coming straight at me. Remember? If I hadn't swerved, they'd be gathering us up in a basket right now. Since when did you start driving?'

'Today. The first day of the rest of my life.'

'How wonderful for you. And original. And just think, it was almost the last, too. How's Rita, is she okay? She's pretty quiet.'

'She's a quiet girl, a good girl, aren't you, honey?'

Rita stared at Liz as though *she* were reading a book, but one that was far beyond her capacity to understand, a horror story in which she had become physically involved, a terrifying script that sprouted arms and drew her into a thicket of inexplicable word and action. Nothing like a breakneck bit of stunt flying and a dip in the lake to waken a deluded and drunken ego – however young and unformed – to a few home truths. This question of her enhanced abilities, well, *really*. What a crock, and she'd been sitting in the very centre of it, manufacturing fantasies and smearing herself with them. Her hand was a small cracked cup that couldn't hold even the dregs of power. Useless. Worthless. What did she think she was doing, and with Liz? She had entrusted the thin thread of her life to a woman who could so carelessly misplace it, or break it. She was the stranger in disguise her real mother had always warned her about. And speaking of mothers, how quickly they get down to business, even the new ones, hanging out the shingle and rubbing their hands briskly together – no pain, no profit. Before their bond was hours old, Liz had strafed her with angry words, had confused and humiliated her, had forced her to kiss Blake Hardy's cold headstone, burdening her with the suffocating weight of *another* dead man.

Stupid, about summed it up, a bucket of a word in which this whole mess of misunderstanding belonged. Rita was chilled and bereaved, shivering in the water, where were her clothes? She didn't remember taking them off, though she can still see her other self leaving her when the car spun out of control, her magnificent and expanded self flying out of the window, drifting away, diffusing in the air. What remained of her was nothing to crow about. Would her parents want it back, this stripped and gnarled thing, unfeeling as a hunk of driftwood? Hardly.

'What the hell were you doing? Taking in the view?'

'*I* was reading, if you want to know. Then I just happened to notice this, I don't know, sort of island in the middle of the road, with corn growing on it and everything. Naturally, I started to drive around it –'

'Wait a minute, Liz, it's my turn. *You* were reading?'

'Yes.'

'While you were driving?'

'Yes. You have a problem with that?'

'Gosh, no. When Burton comes along to divorce his truck from that tree, I'll just tell him you were engaged in literary pursuits, shall I? Must have been pretty fascinating?'

'Oh, but it *was*.'

'Better than loins?' Better than *his* loins? What was Liz doing in Innis's car, anyway, her ridiculous polka dot dress snagged wantonly around the aerial?

'It was *ed*ucational, if you don't mind. Did you know that the Ritz cracker was invented in 1934?'

'Why, *no*, I didn't.'

'There, you see. I picked up quite a bit of handy information, like, about cream cheese, and toothpicks. And human sacrifice, too.'

'How useful. And with toothpicks. What *was* this book?'

'Ruthie, I wouldn't read a book, I've already read several. This was some papers the wind slapped on the windshield, I didn't have any choice. You should have seen this one picture, though, it was real cute. A sort of garden gnome, I guess, but with an enormous head, and a pointy chin, and his mouth gaping open.'

'Sounds like a Stink.'

'And horns ... *say*, who's the male animal slobbering on his paws up there?'

'You mean that mangy, scruffy, flea-bitten excuse for a dog? That's only Dick, ignore him. Too bad, thought I nailed him earlier.'

'You'd think he was human, the way he's ogling that nun.'

'Imagine her throwing off her clothes like that.'

'Imagine us.'

'Do you think we're in shock?'

'She's not. She's having a riot, look, splashing around, standing on her head, nice legs.'

'Liz, what's that in the water?'

'Where, I don't see anything.'

'It was behind her, now it's moving in, toward us. See?'

'A periscope?'

'A watersnake, I bet.'

'Ew! No, wait, it's a –'

'It's a ... a ... hard-on?'

'A *boner! Ew*, I hate those things, get it away from me!'

'Hello, girls.'

'*LaBelle!* Good God, *where* did you come from? And did you have to bring your dildo with you, you scared us half to death.'

'Good, serve you right. This one isn't mine, I don't go in for stone. I found it in the trunk.'

'You were in the trunk the whole time? Rita, it was Granny in the trunk. Remember when I said to you, hey, sounds like there's a dead body rolling around back there?'

'Rita, you hurt?'

'Nah, I'm okay, Granny. Nice to see you. How did you get out of the trunk?'

'My little secret, dear. I'll tell ya later.'

'And what were you doing there, I'd like to know?'

'You would, eh, Liz? How about tellin' us what you were doin', stealin' this kid, sneakin' her out of the hospital. Don't think I wasn't watchin' you right from the start. I don't sleep that much.'

'Liz! You didn't?'

'What?'

'Holy friggin' Jesus, you did. You *kidnapped* Rita, you were leaving with her, weren't you? This is so *sick*, I can't believe it.'

'Lay off, Ruthie. She's my baby. *Don't* you remember, the one they forced me to give away. This is *her*. She's *mine*.'

'Don't *you* remember, it was a *boy?*'

'No, it wasn't.'

'Your sister's cracked, Ruthie. Alls you got to do it take one look at Rita to see she's the spittin' image of her father.'

'Shut up, LaBelle.'

'Not that caretaker guy, but the other one, the stud, Mr Sex-on-Wheels.'

'I said, *shut up.*'

My uncle?

'He was always out at the farm, had his eye on Kim. A real sleazeball. Worse than Tennessee Ernie.'

'Way to go, LaBelle. Nice way to break it to her.'

'What's the big deal? Everyone knows her mother's a whore.'

My uncle my father?

'LaBelle! For God sakes, *enough*. And don't point that thing at me. What are you doing out of the hospital anyway? I thought you were about ready to kick the bucket?'

'Kick ass, more like.'

'Say, isn't that the missing –'

Myunclefatherunclefatheruncle –

'Yeah.'

'But didn't he lose it in the channel?'

'Who knows, maybe he had two. Want it?'

'No, thanks. It's ugly.'

'Tacky.'

'Obscene.'

'It would make a good towel rack.'

'Shower gift.'

'Door stop.'

'Hood ornament.'

'C'mon, girls, do we *need* this thing?'

'Nah. Throw it back.'

'It's too small.'

'No, wait, on second thought, I will take it. Here.'

'*Sold* to the gal with the saddlebags.'

'I do *not* have saddlebags, you old cow.'

'What are those then, Ruthie, mudflaps?'

'Everyone!' Sister St. Anne, plain Anne now, defrocked of her saintly designation, broke the surface with a simple enough question, to which there seemed to be no answer. 'Where's Rita?'

A missing child. Nothing more terrifying, no pain more searing, more numbing. And what parent standing outside of such a loss, gazing sympathetically in, doesn't entertain the guilty and inadmissible thought – *thank God it isn't mine*. Liz was off the hook. She needn't be implicated directly in this, a distance had opened between her and Rita, a chasm over which she could send her concern. Wasn't one loss enough? Hadn't she paid her emotional dues? She can well imagine what the parents will go through if Rita *is* gone, likely drowned. It's not as though she doesn't love Rita anymore, of course she does, she has for years. But she's not her mother. Liz could admit this freely now, finally, with a deep exhalation of relieved and reviving breath. She wasn't the one responsible.

Rita didn't need a rock in each hand, she was dead weight as it was, grey skin creeping over her warm living arm. Watch for the headlines: *Girl Looks Back, Turns to Stone*. Her uncle had done much worse than molest her, he had *fathered* her, he had penetrated and stained every cell in her being. Read all about it, he was not in that battered old house of theirs, but *in* her, fouling her with his blood, his body. As Rita slipped under, black hair raying round her head, she kept her mind focused like an evil and murderous eye on one thought – she would cleanse herself of him for good, she would wash him out of her, she *would*, even if it meant washing out her own life with his. She would take him to the bottom of the lake and hold him under, hold him until the head that was stuck in her head bloated and burst. I'll be all things to him, she thought, the perfect daughter, I'll be his death chamber and death watch and death rattle and death trap.

She might have accomplished it, too, this grisly baptism, if another sacrament hadn't cut in. A wedding, or at least Roger Christopher's discarded gown, whirled by, current-embodied and waltzing with a protean groom, a smoothly muscled and liquid lover, limbs all over and around the bride, heart nowhere in sight.

Well. Soak your head in poetry or theology, then open your eyes under water, it sharpens vision. What Rita saw was an angel, albeit a water-logged one, foundering, collapsing quickly into a flat, jerky dancer, jilted into a rag. An angel that had come to save her, *at long last*, and was now himself in serious trouble. *Chamuel! He can't swim*. Rita kicked her feet wildly and lunged toward him, closing her eyes, holding on tight, tumbling into a shroud of darkness.

Rescued by Rover? Give *us* a break. It was Dick, Dick the Dog, who was the unsung hero, the real guardian angel and headline stealer, crown attorney of the deep, the ravager of garbage cans and generous benefactor of 'said excrement' under foot. *He* was the canine *ex machina* who sank his teeth into the scruff of that wedding gown's neck – Rita's lifeline – and dragged her unconscious body ashore.

Terminal Male

WHEN PERLEN DOAN was a boy he never sat still. Not for a meal, not for a tale – tall or short – not even for a dime. You couldn't pay him to pause. Couldn't stall him with a command, or a honeyed tripwire of a phrase. A hug was a cage out of which he burst with a triumphant laugh on the run. He slept lightly, restless as a swift, his dreams bearing him forward, on and on. Hard to believe that he was now stopped, extinguished, tagged into immobility, the game eddying on without him. Surely there was a way of springing him – alive!

Swallows swooping and a prowling cat and jigging harvestmen and dizzy red mites wove a wreath of life around Perlen. Gladdin Doan did more. He was a doctor after all, and a father, who quickened the stiff and lazy bones of his child into an ongoing idea that flickered here and there, catching in the leaves, sparks in the grass, smouldering on the edge. The reluctant resurrected into a one-man religion. What else could he do? Pretend, like other failed and grieving parents who had let their children slip out of their hands, that such a loss can be borne? Bend to the exhortation that one must heal the wound while accommodating the knife in the chest? *Get on with it?* Gladdin knew his place and his duty, knew his heart, exposed and weathered as he sat patiently day in and out by Perlen's grave. You'd think it was a crèche he minded, and his boy only biding his time, waiting until he gained enough mastery in his legs to leap out and tear away into the wind like a child made of well-tempered and indestructible mettle.

Having tramped a fair path between this world and the next, having picked his arduous way into the unimaginable and back, Gladdin wasn't especially surprised to see a fellow-pilgrim – haggard, bloodied, and bruised – emerge from the woods that skirted the graveyard. The coins had fallen from his eyes and he was naked, except for one finned foot which slapped the ground like a palm whapping a bare belly as he approached.

'Dead, are you?' Gladdin was only mildly curious and making polite conversation.

'Got me. I *feel* dead. You?'

'Neither here nor there.'

'Mmm.'

'Drowned then, did you?'

'How can you tell?'

'Mask squeeze. Nasty welt round your eyes.'

'No … I distinctly recall someone pumping my chest. It was the *ambulance* that did me in.'

'Run you over, did it?'

'Guy thought he was a race car driver. Tires squealing, siren screaming, then the back doors flew open and I got sucked out. Rolled right into the road. Hit my head on a rock. Must have passed out for a while. Someone was washing my face with their hair, long silky hair, and beautiful voice, I remember a woman's voice whispering to me, *Quatro olhos vêem mais que dois*. Haven't a clue what it means, do you? One thing, her breath absolutely *reeked*. I opened my eyes and there was this dog, this ugly spotted mutt drooling into my face like it was a plate of raw hamburger.'

'Sit down, son. Best thing for a dead body. Here, my back's tired. Been giving my boy shoulder rides. Turn around, that's it, let me lean up against you for a bit.'

Back to back, their perspective was complete, theatre in the round, the orbicular view that took in the sweep of the graveyard, the fields beyond, the lake beyond that, the woods on the other side, the road into town. Innis sighed. Gladdin sighed. Not sighs that spoke to each other, mingling in the air above their lightly touching heads, homogenizing into any kind of accord. Gladdin bored a hole through the immediate, gazing so intently into the past, while Innis, lacerated and bereft, his memory and the valuables it contained apparently missing, looked straight ahead of him into the bright undecorated room that held his future. His sigh was a sigh of relief, for he felt incredibly light and unburdened, as though stripped down to his radiant skinny-dipping soul. Glancing around, he became sharply aware of his surroundings, hyper-appreciative of detail, of every wing and blade, veined and ribbed, as though he were somehow responsible for their creation and maintenance. Painstaking, delicate work, but what a spectacle, *what* a delight. His pulse throbbed, a leaping fry in his wrist.

Gladdin broke away from him with a startled jerk. '*You*,' he said, offended, 'your heart is beating.' He struggled to his feet and wandered away, muttering to himself.

Oddball, Innis thought, touching himself tenderly, placing a kind hand over his chest, fond fingers alighting on his neck, his side, searching, exploring. How enchanting, his own nurturing warmth, the responses his body made, his heart banging away, *yes*, his bones snapping and creaking, his breath whistling up one nostril and out the other … he sneezed, he belched, his stomach twanged pitifully like a lone guitar playing the introductory chords to a hurtin' song called *Life*. Yes, he was alive, no doubt about it, he was *starving*.

Innis took in his surroundings once again, but with a more predatory eye, his mystical patronage of the grass and insects forsaken in this hungrier scrutiny. Instantly, he spotted a headstone that was lit up like a diner, encircled with a set of Christmas lights that winked off and on. This was the grave of Neil and Marg Wooley, a hoot in life, humour undiminished in death. How do they *do* that, Innis wondered, walking over to inspect it. A mini white picket fence, an Al Capp whirligig, and, *all right*, a garden containing tomato plants, zucchini, squash. Now here lay a couple who had a healthy and comprehensive understanding of what constituted a plot, a burgeoning green sequel extending the story of their lives. Though on reading the stone, Innis noted that Marg (no deathdate) still had a few rows to hoe in this world before stretching out as marital mulch between the stringbeans and Neil (maybe *he* was the power source for the winking lights). In fact, Marg Wooley took great pride in this garden, lavishing as much care on it as she once did on her husband, killing him off slowly, mind you, with her lethal melt-in-your-mouth crusts. Death by pastry. Marg was Dolly Stink's fiercest rival in the fall fair's 'Rude Root' competition, and herein lay the tantalizing horticultural evidence: vegetal entendres grotesque and suggestive, grossly elongated parsnips, engorged carrots drooping hilariously at the ends, prosthetic ready-to-wear potatoes and turnips. The mimicry and mockery of the vegetable kingdom writ large and lewd. All Innis saw was lunch. He stepped eagerly over the picket fence, snapped himself off a hefty zucchini, and was about to set to, when someone shouted, 'Hey! *You!*' His fingers clenched guiltily around the pilfered item, and he turned quickly to explain – his hunger, his disoriented state – a nervous smile notched in his face, his flipper whisked off his heel and held before him like a mutant fig leaf. He saw a nun running toward him, something clenched in *her* hand that looked suspiciously cocked and loaded.

Not her. And *armed*. His recollections weren't so scattered that he didn't know who *she* was, the hospital's resident hobgoblin and mischief-maker, pouring the contents of the patients' bedpans straight into their juice glasses, cracking open penicillin capsules like hummingbird eggs and pirouetting the magic powder into a spiral galaxy around her head. Innis held up the zucchini defensively, as if to ward her off with a prophylactic charm. 'Get thee to a nunnery,' he croaked, desperate. It *was* all he could think of, but it didn't stop the black-and-white, too too solid apparition from charging at him, an assassin's cold light in her eye. '*Aaaaaaaa*,' he screamed. Which startled her. She tripped over Newt Pringle's jutting footstone, and the weapon shot out of her hand like a missile, hitting the Wooleys' tombstone with a loud *crack*, smashing two of the Christmas lights (the set winked out), and engraving a huge pock in the angel's face that smiled benevolently down on Neil's not-so-vital statistics.

'Crap,' she said, hobbling over to Innis. 'It broke. Damn!'

It wasn't her.

'You could try crazy glue. Just don't stick your eyelids to your cheeks, like Tennessee Ernie did. He thought it was Murine.'

Innis stared at this strange woman, then down at the grey stone object that lay shattered at his feet, then back at her again. 'What is it?' he asked finally.

'Don't give me that. You know damn well what it is.'

'I do?'

'Yes, *you do*. And I went to a lot of trouble to find you after you'd buggered off, so I could give it to you. So smarten up.'

'I'm sorry, I'm just not myself. I had this accident, well, several, and then I hit my head, and … I can't seem to remember anything.'

'Amnesia, eh?'

'Yeah, that's it.'

'Bullshit.'

'Huh?'

'Pathetic. What, you see that on Bugs Bunny, or something?'

'No, really, it's true.'

'Yeah? When was the Ritz cracker invented?'

'1934. Why?'

'Who's your least favourite cousin twice removed on your mother's side?'

'Angusena Welch.'

'Who am I?'

'Ruthie Stink?'

'Who are you?'

'Innis C. George.'

'What's that?'

'A flipper.'

'And *that*?'

'A zucchini.'

'Prize winner.'

'It's a big one.'

'So?'

'Yes, you're right. I was faking it. Almost had myself convinced, though.'

'Too bad about your cock.'

'Oh, *that*. Doesn't matter, it's a fake, too. Look how easily it broke. Like Inch's research, nine-tenths invention.'

'By the way, your car's in the drink again. Can't understand why you let Liz drive it.'

'I didn't. *Blast*, again? Your sister's a menace. And she ripped me off for twenty bucks, too.'

Ah. Good.

'How long have you been a nun?'

'About an hour. We all switched clothes. Great, isn't it?' Ruthie sucked in her cheeks, struck a pose, and strutted down a mossy hump (Edgar Wilmott 1902-1956), as though it were a catwalk. 'I'd always wanted to be a nun. Well, for about a week, anyway. When most girls were getting their periods, I got my vocation. Didn't last, though. Like your amnesia.'

'Yeah, corny, eh? But that's what *I've* always wanted to be. Light. Free. No personal clutter, no clawing memories, no expectations from wheedling parents. Or children.'

'No Stinks.'

'Exactly. Ruthie?'

'I'm listening.'

'I'm leaving. Today, right now, before this place really is the death of me. Why don't you come along? We'd be fabulous together. And think, no ties, no responsibilities. You wouldn't have to wash another dish, or for that matter, *throw* another dish, for the rest of your life.'

She *was* listening. Go on.

'What do you have to look forward to here? More kids, a brood of Stink brats? A mobile home in the field next to the pig pen? Black eyes and split lips from your moron of a husband? Then before you know it you're celebrating your fiftieth wedding anniversary, when the family presents you with a kitschy doll dressed in fifty one-dollar bills. Your big payoff for a lifetime in the trenches.'

'But I've seen those, they're sweet. And what's wrong with a mobile home, they're very nice. Have you ever been *inside* one?'

'Listen, I came here looking for something made of stone, an effigy, cold, dead, and as it turns out, nonexistent. But that doesn't matter, because I found you. A vigorous, hot-blooded, exciting –'

'Slut.'

'Really? Prove it.'

'Say, where's your flipper?'

'Look up, way up.' And there it was, waggling comically in the air, a flapping rubber tongue telling an old joke that only gravity got.

Who was chasing who, feet pounding like heartbeats over the ordered dead? Innis dodged around gravestones, Ruthie hopped over top of them, skirts held high, hair streaming. She lunged, he evaded, he grasped, she ducked away. High spirits shrieked through them, snapping out of fingertips. They began knocking over gravestones. Markers thudded to the ground like bodies dropping. A crack shot up the face of one stone, a deep branching rift that sundered birthdate from deathdate, splitting open the hyphen – life the briefest of dashes. Above them, unnoticed, black clouds were building. Soon, a vandalizing wind streaked through, tearing at the trees and yanking savagely at Ruthie's habit. She tried to tackle Innis and he skipped away, light as a torn leaf, and stretched himself out seductively on the cracked stone. He smiled, ready to pelt off the moment she got close, but she moved faster than he did this time and grabbed him by the ankle, twisting his arm behind his back.

'Ow! Let go. This how you guys make love here?'

'Yeah, and there's more.' Ruthie crawled over him, pinching and poking.

'Stop *that*. It's too hard.'

'No, it isn't. You call *that* hard?'

'Don't get personal. I mean this gravestone. Let's shift down to the grass.'

'I like it here. Let's *do* it.'

Naughty, naughty. The weather *didn't like* anyone stealing its thunder. A lightning bolt shot across the sky. The wind cackled in their ears, raked their soles. Tried to insinuate itself, making a rift between their entwined and shuddering bodies. Finally – an old trick – it flicked a squiggle of something into Ruthie's open eye as she stared down absently at the stone's script, raying out from behind Innis's head.

Suddenly she sat up, pushing him roughly aside.

'What's wrong? Something bite you?'

Ruthie didn't even seem to hear him, but leaned back, blinking, transfixed.

'What, you leave a roast in the oven?'

'I have to go.' She jumped up, smoothed the rumpled habit modestly over her legs, and turned quickly away. 'Goodbye.'

'Wait!' Innis was stunned. 'Don't go. *Please*. What did I do?'

'Nothing.'

'I don't get it.'

'You're light, remember? Free.' She was hustling toward the road, but then stopped, and called back, 'What does the "C" stand for?'

'What?'

'In your name.' She had to shout it against the bucking wind. 'You know, Innis *C.* George?'

'Cnut.'

'Pardon *me?*'

'CNUT!' *Cnut?*

Ruthie sucked in her breath and set her jaw at a murderous angle. What she heard, distorted by the wind, the letters cunningly tumbled, the name altered, was an insult coming crude and cruel from the lips of a sexually disappointed man.

'Well, same to you, *stud* bunny,' she bellowed, annoyed with herself for not coming up with a more cutting gibe. And while she was at it, how *dare* he? *Gram is not a moron*, she thought, loyalty striking hard, as she stormed away, a dark eddy scorching down the road, *He has these dreamy Stink eyes that look right back at you* ...

At this moment, Innis wished he could think of some suitably tragic figure to identify with, some forsaken and unjustly abused hero. But he was bankrupt, resourceless, as stripped of identities as he was of clothing. Besides, this weather was insane. If he tried to rage on *this* heath, his mouth would fill like a dipper, his lungs like barrels. Death was in every drop of water that slammed into him, every drop hammering him into this burying ground. Desperately, he cast about for something, *anything*, to cover and protect himself with. He clutched at a bank of greenery and ripped out two verdant and abundant handfuls that he held up before him like green torches, the beacons of a bit part player making his way up the ranks (and into town), slowly and certainly as Birnam wood sneaks across the stage to Dunsinane.

Gladdin Doan opened his eyes in the mudhole of an open grave, water slapping his cheeks, shushing in his ears, and he understood that he was back in the war. He heard the explosives detonating, the crack of rifles firing. Drumming rain, as usual. But no stench. No water-treading rats, bobbing shit, bloated rotting mates bumping gently against him – odd. He peered out over the trench and saw a young man standing idle a few yards away, hands in his pockets, biding his time. Good Lord. 'Get down, hit the dirt!' Gladdin warned. *Damn fool.* He climbed out of the trench, how could he not risk it? He was not so inured to death that he wanted to see this careless boy blown to bits. As he stumbled out, the young man raised his healthy handsome face to him, and smiled in instant recognition. *Glory!* It was *Perlen!* Gladdin staggered, following the jagged streaking path the lightning made, searing his feet as he walked, galvanizing him with the keenest of anticipation for this moment that he had been searching and searching for, and that finally lay before him clear as day. As he approached this undiminished marvel, *his son*, Gladdin saw with relief how settled Perlen was in this new maturity, no longer restless, but a grown man, his arms a calm and perfect haven for a weary old one to sink into.

The Cobweb Theory

Je pleure, il pleut, je pleure, il pleut, was what the rain said to Rita weeping against her windowpanes. A language she understood no matter how rapidly it was spoken.

Failure, it might as well have said, knitting the web of accusation in which she struggled. Had she escaped from this house? No. Cut her family ties? No. Found Emmy Stink or even a girlfriend for Holmes? No. Saved Chamuel? No no *no*.

Forget, forget. The rain was multilingual, and speaking more gently than she would acknowledge, absolving her, a million wet tongues laving the house.

'Did you save me?' Rita asked Holmes earlier, while she was bundled on the living room couch and her parents tiptoed around the kitchen whispering in a happy domestic conspiracy, making sandwiches and coffee for their guest.

'We all did, Rita. Of course Dick did the most important thing of all, dragging you ashore. Then everybody pitched in, Anne, LaBelle, those crazy Stronghills, Dr Nopper, your folks, me. No possible way were we going to lose *you.*'

'Even Liz?'

'Especially Liz. She wasn't trying to hurt you. Just got her wires crossed. As usual.'

'You think you'll marry her?'

'*Geez.*' His hand flew to his chest, shielding his heart. 'What a notion, don't scare me like that.'

Was he serious? She couldn't tell. 'I didn't do anything for you, Holmes. Didn't do anything right. Because I'm a moron, that's why. A pinhead, a *pea*brain.'

'Hey, don't be inferiotic.'

'Inferiotic? That's pretty good.'

'You think that's good, listen to this.' Holmes furled his fingers, making a megaphone of his hand, then rolled an announcer's large print voice down it, giving birth to: 'ARTIFICT'.

'Wow. What's it mean?'

Holmes beamed with pride, father of the word. 'Don't know,' he said. 'That is, I'm still working on the definition.'

'What d'you have so far?'

'Okay, here goes. **artifict** (ar'ti-fikt), n.[L. *ars, artis,* skill, art + *fictio,* a making, counterfeiting], 1. a fact that isn't true. 2. any object excavated out of dreams, fiction, etc. 3. an imaginary vegetable, resembling a cucumber, only longer.'

'I'm not so sure about the third one.'

'No? I want it to have range, though. A sort of Neopolitan flavour?'

'But I do like it. Really, it shines.' And it did, glinting like a holy medal as she turned it over and over examining it. Perhaps she could use it to exorcise that other word, the bad one that had taken root, thorny and dark, striking deep in her head. 'Holmes?'

'That's me.'

'What does "whore" mean?'

'Depends who's saying it?'

'Granny Stink called my mother that. A whore.'

'That's easy, then. It means someone who wanted a child so badly they had to go about it in a different sort of way. Break a few rules, get more of the family involved, like how Stinks do things. It was probably a compliment.'

'I don't think so, Holmes. But thanks.'

Rita watched as her parents emerged out of the bright kitchen, carrying the refreshments. They bustled in, smiling and awkward, pleased as children who have seized the reins of home economy in their delighted and untutored hands. As Sofia offered Holmes a cup, coffee sloshed over the side and spilled, making for one more sibling splat in a large extended family of brownish-red stains on the rug. She held up her hand, whispering behind it to him, but the secret she wanted to convey sloshed over that as well, and everyone heard. 'I slipped a bit of wine into it,' she said. 'And gin.'

Now here was a combination he'd never tried. Invention was in the air.

From her bed, Rita scanned the contents and corners of her room, sight veering cautiously into the closet. No footloose dead man's boots. No fantastic beings born of clothes mated in the dark. Chamuel and her uncle both in irretrievable exile. Not that she wanted to be terrified out of sleep, haunted, dogged, but this dimness, flatness, blankness was equally alarming. It struck her, studying her unremarkable room, that they had taken something valuable of hers with them. Something she hadn't realized she possessed that was bound up with them, as much a part of their bodies, their thin skin, as it was of hers. Thieves. And they'd gotten away with it, slipping through her cracked hand and leaving only a mirror-calm and impenetrable surface behind.

She knew that what Holmes had told her before leaving, reeling through the door, expansive on her mother's brew, was connected with what the rain was saying, pattering its advice, laying it like a soft garment on the roof all around.

Let go, let go.

'You know, Rita, I don't believe anymore that the dead *want* to be remembered. They stick us with all their old junk, even their funny names, and disappear into a few feet of real estate heaped with nice anonymous earth.'

'Unreal estate,' Rita mused. 'Is *that* an artifact?'

Holmes laughed, and the rain did, too, lightening up.

Rita sat up and switched on the Blessed Virgin. Switched her off, on, off again. *Click, click,* faster and faster, transforming her from a visionary presence to a strobe light, a little miracle of electricity, the sacred manifesting itself on demand. Victor had surprised Rita with this gift after supper, a Virgin Mary lamp in a shoe box. He had given it to his daughter in private gratitude to Mary herself for favours rendered, and in further supplication to extend those favours, to keep night terrors out of Rita's room, to keep her safe and blessed amply, if not with faith, then with hope. And Rita was yet young enough to be thrilled, and to find this lambent gift beautiful. *Not yet* would she excommunicate the Mother of God, relegating her to a dusty purgatorial back shelf, all for the sin of being tacky. As it was, Rita held out her hands and bathed them in Mary's lovely blue radiance, letting the beneficent light flow down the winding scar that laced around her fingers, the fine line that held her together. She studied her hands, in wonder, for they seem to have aged in advance of her. How would she ever catch up with them? And would she, with them, ever catch anything worth holding?

The bed creaked as she stood up, speaking, as beds always do, in complaint. *Stop worrying. Be a kid. Cripes.* Cautiously, still incredulous, Rita approached her second surprise of the evening, the one her mother had given her. This one was the best because it had come

straight out of the blue, *impossible*, but there it was – a snake curled in
its water dish in the bottom of a glass cookie jar. Nothing Rita knew
about her mother predicted this gift. Where had it come from, her
ability to give something so unusual, so unlike Sofia and Sofia's
notions of what a daughter should want, something that probably
terrified her? The snake itself Rita had forgotten about, locked in her
lunchbox the day she ran off to her final, and transfiguring, initiation. Stu Stink dropped the lunchbox off at her place. It would have
hurt his lovelorn eyes to see it sitting empty as a craw by Rita's desk
the next day. Rita could certainly imagine her mother's shock when
she flipped open the lid, but her imagination didn't give her any free
rides from that chaotic scene, the screaming, the broom smashing
the box to bits, to the one where her mother is gently force-feeding
the snake capsules of chopped mouse because it won't eat. ('*You*
chopped a mouse?') All the time Rita was in the hospital, Sofia
nursed the snake, spoiled it even, her well-kept secret. It developed
ulcers on its gums, so she swabbed its mouth twice a day with hydro-
gen peroxide. When it moulted, she made sure that its transparent
eyecaps came off with the skin (which she saved because it resembled
a peek-a-boo Barbie evening gown). She decorated its home with
reptilian taste, including a jokey pipe-smoking picture of St. Patrick,
doodled horns and moustache, taped like wallpaper to one side of
the jar.

'How did you know what to do with him?'

'I called your teacher. He was very helpful. A smart guy. Too bad
he's gone.'

'Mr Christopher? Gone?'

'I forgot to tell you. He took off. The school board is furious.
Anyway, he left me this book. See.'

'*You* did all this stuff?'

'Sure. Isn't he worth it? Aren't you?'

Well, *he* was. He was so-o-o pretty. Patrick, she called him, carrying the joke further, crowning him with it, Patrick with the golden
eyes, and the yellow racing stripe down his black suit, and his shiny
toffee-coloured chin, and his flicking kinder-than-breath tongue.
But she wasn't going to keep him. Not after watching him all afternoon trying to solve the puzzle of captivity. This day and every day,
probing and pushing, rubbing his nose tirelessly against the glass
walls of the jar, as though he had simply misplaced his freedom,

momentarily lost the key to it that only Rita held. *Let go. Let go.* A glass cage, a Christian name, a pair of loving hands – soon he'd whistle through them all, swimming back into the blue.

Rita yawned and climbed back into bed. *Sheesh. Get some sleep.* The rain was falling softly, persuasively, advancing some bleeding heart theory about amity and accord. And since we're all in this together, was the gist of it, let's not equivocate, let's not differ ... let's *party*.

Tit for Tat

THE HERO WAS in the doghouse. The hero was *chained* to the doghouse. See spotted Dick sit. Immobile. Stewing in a boiling black kettle of disgrace. *Wool of bat, and tongue of dog*, indeed. Dethroned. Unking'd. Hear him groan, sigh, whimper, and yelp, gnawing on the bitter flank of injustice. Self-pity was not the word. Sorrow was not even the word. *Dog dirt* was the word, and he'd been dealt it in spades. His favoured place by the stove, *usurped*. The upturned crown of his dogdish, *empty*. Even his fleas had deserted him, pledging fealty to his successor, the traitorous progeny of his own *loins*, the double-dealing two-faced Prince.

A lamentable tale. A tragedy as yet to reach its climax, for he had heard evil rumours, treasonous talk of 'putting him down,' as though he were a one-dog rebellion, and not the rightful king of canines deposed. Had he not *saved* a child's life? A credit to his moral coffers that surely, *surely* hadn't been cancelled out by that other insignificant withdrawal, that mere flap of flesh he'd so neatly removed from between Baby Stink's legs. What a scene! Talk about comic relief. Baby Stink shrieking and wailing like the little whey-faced coward he is, and Ruthie hysterical, 'My *baby*, oh my baby! Castrated! Oh my *God!*' Dick hadn't seen so much ham in action since his last visit to the pig pen. Then Prince, barking and barking, most deviously, a hollow and opportunistic complaint, serving himself to his father's future. As it turned out, Dick had only circumcised the kid. He'd done them all a favour. Think of all those nasty diseases he might have gotten, did Stinks ever wash? He should send them a doctor's bill. But what does he get instead? *This*. Exile. Prison, doghouse arrest, with a villain no doubt waiting in the wings to do him in, *to fill another room in hell*. Tell you one thing, not with this dog's body. If Dick had to bury his dagger-sharp teeth into something, it definitely wasn't going to be the ground.

'A dose of his own medicine.'

'Eye for an eye.'

'Paid in kind.'

'Measure for measure.'

Wearing nothing but a Band-Aid and diaphanous dried tears –

the aforementioned Prince loosely accessorized, flying at his heels –
Baby Stink zipped through the crowd, dodging in and out, a long
squeal of pleasure issuing out of his mouth, a trailing vocal banner
that whipped the dog into a dancing frenzy and made everyone's ear-
drums throb like tom-toms. Baby had taken a swig of hundred-proof
excitement distilled from the celebratory air. Now this was a *party!* A
love feast. The fiftieth wedding anniversary of Granny and Grampa
Stink, a 'weeding' anniversary as LaBelle insisted on calling it. But
think, *fifty* years, a top-heavy five-decker scoop of time that took a
county of friends and relations to savour. Even the livestock were
invited. *Even* the Stronghills.

From Dick's disadvantage point on the periphery of the event, a
discordant jungle-growth of sound rose around the main house and
garden, language sprouted ornate limbs and caught in its twining
embrace this blatting and braying and fertile excess. A roar to Dick.
But a roar of life, its very voice, from which he was excluded. He
pricked up his ears, hoping to tune in at least a familiar intonation, a
clement and forgiving drawl. With luck someone might sing his
praises, graft his good name like a pure note onto this raucous medley, earn him a reprieve. But soft! What's this?

'His *dick?*'

'Worst case I've ever seen.'

'Poison ivy, you say?'

'Covered the entire genital area. This festering, weeping rash.
Looked like he was wearing calamine underwear.'

'That's awful.'

'Some woman from down below came to pick him up. She
thought it was pretty funny.'

Dr Nopper slid his hands into his pockets and wandered over to
the garage sale table that was manned, so to speak, by Tennessee
Ernie. The set-up was LaBelle's brainchild, her efficient, if ruthless,
method of winnowing out the useless anniversary presents – 'Who
wants this *crap?*' As he examined the three-foot Don Ameche bust,
and the velvet painting of a fondling naked couple, Dr Nopper
recalled other Stink parties he'd attended, and how they really did
need a medic on hand when they threw one, for they took the verb to
heart. Their parties were not only thrown, but rolled, punched,
kicked, tossed, and blown wide open. Already he's attended to Baby
Stink (that dog did a better job than most interns), and Chet, who'd

nearly given himself a concussion by playing a particularly vigorous rendition of *Moon River*. He'd extracted a fruitfly that was sailing on the curve of Frank Stronghill's eyeball – a shifting constellation of them was moving through the party in orbit around an overripe Stink aunt – and he'd plucked a sliver out of Meg Swit's tongue.

'Got it from one of Dolly's lumber muffins,' she said, once her tongue had been released from his medical grip and flapping freely again.

'Not really.'

'Yeah, she sweeps up the workshop floor and dumps it in the batter. My sister Lorna got a drill bit in hers.'

Not really. But the licked and glistening evidence lay before him, on offer along with the rejected anniversary presents – available at half price to their original donors – and a few Stink collectibles: some burnt-out lightbulbs, a quart basket of rusty wing nuts from Burton's Tool Museum, Dinky's cast-off crutches, and the doll which had been presented earlier to LaBelle wearing a green dress made of fifty crisply pleated and tucked dollar bills that was now stripped down to her plastic pudendum. Also, Tennessee Ernie's magic kit in a bashed, taped-up box.

'I'm surprised to see this here. You're not packing it in, are you?'

'I don't believe in magic no more.'

'No?'

'Nope. It's tricks, Doc, that's all. It's not real. Dolly said if I set fire to her curtains one more time she was gonna cream me. Anywho, I ordered a guitar from Eaton's and me and my brothers are gonna start up a band.'

'Couple of guys I knew in medical school did that. Folk music, though. Called themselves the Duo Denims. Clever, eh?'

'I don't get it.'

'How much is this?'

Dr Nopper picked up a transistor radio and checked it out. Looked dandy, he thought, when something lodged in the selector window caught his eye. A cockroach. He turned the dial and with the tuner wand scooted the insect along, chasing it through easy listening, and up through country, jamming it into the far end of the window where it wriggled helplessly. *Plu-ease reeelese mee, let me go-o-o ...*

'Two bucks, plus a quarter for the roach. No kidding, Doc, you got hours of entertainment value right there.'

'I suppose.'

'He who hesitates is lost.'

'What if it's full of roaches?'

'Geez, yeah. Maybe *I'll* buy it. Here.'

Sauntering away from the table with a lighter step, a wealthier man, Dr Nopper felt that bubbling surge of delight which contact with the wayward waters of Stink rationale usually brought him. Stinks. How corrosive they were, eating away at whatever held you firm and in place. A family with undertow. A human concoction spiked with a cold dissolving current. Addictive. They slaked a thirst, almost. Look at Ruthie Stink over by the beer fridge they'd hauled out onto the lawn. Her hands roughly and affectionately frisking Gram as if searching for some clue concealed on his person as to *why* and *how* and *what next*. Dot. Dot.

Dot. Unmistakable, those red splashes in the dust at his feet. Ellipses written in blood. This might bring him, at least, to what was next. A nosebleed? A gash in someone's side, a party casualty too inebriated to notice? He followed the erratic sanguinary path, a randomly linked chain he had to ravel, as was his duty, to tell like beads in a scattered rosary. His blade-sharp nose cut through a thicket of conversation, slitting it open.

'St. Uncumber?'

'What d'you think of this new priest?'

'Some kinda weather, eh? Lots of damage out at the boneyard. Gravestones knocked over, one of 'em cracked right in two.'

'St. Uncumber. He's the one you invoke for tiresome husbands.'

'Whatever happened to that nun?'

'Lightning bolt clean through his head.'

'The teacher.'

'Poison oak was what I heard. Guess the thing swole up to twice its size.'

'I dunno, but they found that polka dot dress she was wearing tangled up with Father Finn's vestments in the confessional.'

'Gladdin Doan?'

'So what's he do with 'em? The husbands? Sounds more like a mafia don than a saint.'

'Doesn't he remind you of somebody?'

'Did you say missionary, or missionary position?'

'No, that was a heart attack. Poor old guy.'

'Spitting image.'

'Rest his soul.'

'Could be his twin brother.'

'St. Uncumber?'

'Roger Christopher?'

'Sofia!'

'Hello, Doctor. Nice to see you.'

'My dear, you must have spent a bundle at the garage sale table. Your purse is mortally wounded. See.'

'What? Damn, I forgot. I threw a steak in my purse before we came over. For their dog. Where is he, have you seen him?'

'Dick? Out back, chained to the dog house.'

'Tsk. He's a *good* dog, he saved Rita's life.'

'A most *noble* creature.'

(If music be the food of … did someone say *steak*?)

'Better give him this. See you, Doctor.'

That medical mystery solved and another leaping into view, chasing the squealing Baby Stink, black hair tossed into knots, a smear of ketchup circling her mouth, a bottle of cream soda in one hand, a bottle of orange crush in the other. Who was this stilt-walking sling-shooting stone-flinging snake-loving (and liberating) two-fisted drinker?

'Hey Rita! What's the effin' idea? You got *taller*.'

'So did you Dinky.'

'Headin' for six feet. See ya there.'

Diagnosis: a kid. A girl child. No cure, she'll grow out of it.

'Say, I'll buy one of those drinks from you, Rita.'

'Here, Dr Nopper, have one. They're free.'

'I insist.'

'Gee, thanks. *Two* dollars.'

'And twenty five cents.'

'Wow, thanks again.'

I have officially passed the buck, thought Dr Nopper, seizing a chair, and settling down to catnap and to await the inevitable. Stinks don't mince their words. After all, this *was* a bash. Slipping into doctor dreams, he pulled up a counterpane of flesh, the fine stitching of veins, *this is my body, this is my bed*.

Holmes watched Rita zip past, the rag of a red bill in her hand, a strip torn off his heart it could be. He'd give her that, gladly. But, nah. The flag she was flying was only money, the Queen smiling as she fluttered by, devil in her pink hair.

'I have something for you, Holmes.'

'Liz, hey. What's this? It's not my anniversary.'

'I made you a pair of pants. Look. To cover your, um, loins.'

'Aren't they covered already?"

'I *think* so. Judging from what I can see. I made them extra roomy in case your loins are, well, you know, in case they need it. I wouldn't want them to feel cramped.'

'And yellow. My fourth favourite colour. Aw, Liz.'

'You like the stripes?'

'Like them? They're magnificent. The perch will be jealous.'

Oh boy, Liz could see it all now. Herself, hostess of the Blue Room, pouring martinis, wending and diffuse, out of a round-bellied Waterford pitcher (wedding present), while Holmes took a turn in the garden walking the sunfish, his yellow pants billowing. Liz glowed (her mother glowered, *another* Stink in the family), flush as the two-dollar bill that Rita spread on Tennessee Ernie's palm (plus twenty-five cents guitar tax), laying that particular circulating bit of royalty to rest. She bought a huge sheaf of papers, a whole crinkled water-cured armful, that Tennessee Ernie said contained the secrets of the universe, a treasure map, an ancient cure for crabs ('torch the suckers'), and more dirty pictures than any kid could hope to find in a stack of *National Geographics*. The first few pages, scanned, were dry as dust, but Rita was sure that Holmes would find something fascinating in it. Where was he though? Only a moment before she'd seen him talking to Liz Stronghill, who was now standing alone, absorbed in a dream, snatching at vagrant floating olives in her head.

'Hi, Liz.'

'Rita, dear. You okay?'

'Yeah, I'm great.'

'Still friends?'

'Of course. You know what I think, Liz?'

'That I should be shot?'

'No. I think you'll make somebody a really good mother. Some baby, you know.'

'*Yeah*? You really think so?'

Aha! She suspected as much. In fact, she *knew* it. She *was* mother material after all, voluminous and soft, enfolding. She couldn't wait to tell Holmes, the prospective father, but when Liz returned to her fantasy, he was gone, having snuck away into the dark skirt of the lake, and not even a glimmer of him remained.

That *two-timing* Holmes. He was actually out back of the house, his face slathered in kisses. Dick was laying them on, wet and thick, with the trowel of his tongue, intending to plaster, bejewel, and stud this fellow-creature's loyal and shining countenance with the gems of his gratitude and affection. Holmes had retrieved the old skeleton key from his pocket and fit its unknown past perfectly into Dick's imprisoning present, opening it up like a field into which Dick tore, running in manic widening circles, air streaming like alcohol into his open mouth. He bounded back and leapt into Holmes's arms like a euphoric panting lover.

'Take it easy, Dick, settle down. I owed you a jail break, remember? What in the devil have you been eating?'

'Holmes.'

'Rita, old pal. Look what Dick's been feasting on, a meal fit for a king.'

'My dinner.'

'Ah.'

'That's okay, Dick. You deserve it. And guess what? My parents said you can come live with us! What do you think of that? Want to?'

Want to? Holy hell, did Pope Clement VI have a mistress, and was he Catholic? How to express the affirmative – was it one wag or two – when communication was so difficult? But oh, he'd flog his answer unmistakably, supply an articulate gross of them, let his hinder if not better half speak for him – *yes, yes, yes*.

'Better pack your briefcase, Dick. Let's see, a couple of bones, this one looks suspiciously feline, what's left of the steak, a pair of yellow pants, and you want me to include those research papers you're hugging, Rita?'

'I thought you might want them.'

'Nope. Besides, they were Dick's in the first, um, second, well, *third* place. Finder's keepers.'

'You know that guy?'

'Innis?'

'Yeah. Was he for real?'

'You think we made him up? He *was* hard to credit, and that's a fact.'

'Holmes, Stu has cotton candy. Maybe we can find some that doesn't have bugs in it.'

'And Ruthie has an announcement to make, wouldn't want to miss that.'

'Who's that with her?'

'The new priest. Father O'Whatsisname.'

'He looks really familiar.'

'I think we better have a closer look. Let's infiltrate, shall we?'

'Meaning?'

Good question when enemy lines had become so entangled that you might see a Stink spitting in his palm and then clasping the hand of a Stronghill, sealing some bargain that for the moment at least held firm. Just try to intrude like dissension between Ruthie Stink and her mother, Grace. What with their tight reconciliatory embrace and the crossfire of apology, it was downright dangerous, each equally determined to take the blame for the breach, filling it with a scattershot confessional spray of hard self-denouncing words. Surely this event was too chummy, altogether too lovey-dovish. Where was the loophole, spyhole, the ditch to snipe down, the forking path of discord? Maybe it was idling in that note tucked in Grampa Stink's pocket that he forgot to read and that Dolly will discover weeks later when she's frisking his smelly motheaten suit jacket for the missing egg money: *Dear John* (not his name). *I'm leaving you, you old shit. I'm running away with that little Italian what dug the well. I only got one you-know-what, but he don't care. Happy Anniversary (ha ha). LaBelle.*

Snoops beware. Back off. Cover your ears. Don't listen! It might not be healthy to hear what Ruthie Stink has to say, climbing up on an overturned trough, clearing her throat, casting into the din her dampening stare, so that conversation goes out like light in people's mouths.

'Friends,' she began ominously. 'Neighbours and family members. And Stinks (a special category). I'd like to welcome to our community, our new priest, Father –'

'It *is* him, isn't it?'

'... and celebrate Granny and Grampa's special day –'

'Where *is* LaBelle, anyway?'

'... by announcing the baptism, here, by special dispensation (mine), of our son Baby Stink. Do you have him, Gram?'

'Sure do, Nits. Got 'im in a headlock. Stop kicking, you.'

'Bare bottom and all.'

'Disgraceful.'

'I'm afraid we'll have to use the birdbath for the ceremony, but Father here says it's probably not the first time it's been used for this sort of thing.'

'Chet used to piss in it.'

'Father *who*?'

'Must be some kinda joke.'

'So what are you callin 'im?'

'Pardon me, Burton?'

'What's his name gonna be?'

'Yes, well, I've decided, that is, Gram and I have agreed to give him the name of a boy who died in the war.'

'Awwwww.'

'A stranger?'

'Touching.'

'A *dead* stranger?'

'Damned unlucky, I'd say.'

'So?'

'Yes?'

'*What is it?*'

'We're calling him –'

And here there was an audible intake of breath, a sea of air sucked in and held in blue-gilled communal suspense.

'*Etzel.*'

Say that again. *Etzel*? Faces registered surprise as though suddenly poked. Eyebrows leapt and lips performed an alphabet of contortions. Everyone considered the name as a body might regard a newsprung feature, a knob or digit or carbuncle that hadn't existed the day before, but was now annoyingly and palpably present. Wasn't there something angular about it, uneven, ill-fitting? Would a saint wear it? *Had* a saint worn it? Who had ever heard of this soldier? Found it in the graveyard? What's wrong with John? Or Peter? Surely it was a mistake. She read the eroded letters incorrectly. That was it. A mistake.

But no, Baby Stink slipped into his new name with a delighted ease, in much the same way that Rita's little pet slipped out of his. Out of the captivity of Patrick, out of *natrix sipedon*, out of snake. When Rita released him from her pocket and into the Stinks' field, how swiftly he vanished, whispering away into his essential self, wearing a smile cousin to the one that graced Baby Etzel's own face.

'He likes it.'

Done!

'It's a good name. Yeah. Etzel Hank.'

'Etzel King, you mean?'

'I said Etzel *Hank*.'

'Etzel Elmer is lovely, you have to admit.'

'Etzel *Waylon*, and I'm the father.'

'No, you're not.'

'What d'ya mean by *that*?'

'Etzel Pretzel.'

'Clam up, Stu.'

'You gonna make me?'

Oh God! Ruthie had to stop this, this steady thrumming drumbeat – where was it coming from? – that was growing louder and louder. *Stinks!* Stink heartbeats accelerating, Stink fingers twitching and Stink jaws clenching, and Stink insults beginning to dive and swoop perilously close.

'Everybody,' she said, 'listen, don't *do* this. Quit it! Right now, this very minute, and I *mean* it. Will you all just *listen!*'

Ruthie searched the heated shifting crowd, desperate for an ally, a calm and controlling voice to join her own, but the priest was laughing, and Dr Nopper was reaching resolutely for his black bag, and Holmes was nowhere to be seen, and even the ancient Janus-faced font, murky rainwater in its hollowed pate, was staring behind and beyond her, its collective eyes and ears and mouths stopped with stone.

His Confession

BLESS ME FATHER for I have sinned. (A lot.) It has been three weeks since my last confession. (A lie.) These are my sins: two tomatoes, a zucchini, a package of pork loin, lightbulbs ... oops, sorry Father, wrong list. *These* are my sins: I was vain. I took the Lord's name. I coveted my mother (though not my father, you kidding). I honoured my neighbour's wife ...

Acknowledgements

My heartfelt thanks to David Burr for all his help, so genially given, for his constancy and his unquestioning belief in this whole endeavour, and to John Metcalf, lavish in his encouragements, witty, sharp-eyed and passionate, the *best* of editors. As well, I want to thank my sister-in-law, Karen MacIntyre, for her computer expertise, and my neighbour, Joan Barfoot, for her enthusiastic support and word sleuthing skills. And special thanks to my son, Sandy, for the many words of his own coinage he has shared with me ('inferiotic' being one), and for his presence. As he so wonderfully puts it, 'I am part of you come true.'

For my own Virgin researches, I am indebted to Marina Warner's *Alone of All Her Sex: The Myth and Cult of the Virgin Mary*. The epigraph is taken from *Seeing Things* ('Lightenings, viii') by Seamus Heaney and is reprinted here with permission of Faber and Faber, London.

Also, I would like to express my gratitude to the Canada Council and the Writers' Reserve Programme of the Ontario Arts Council for their financial support.

Quatro olhos vêem mais que dois? Two heads are better than one.